The Young Male's Marriage Primer

Power Tools for a Successful Marriage

By
Larry Danby

New York

The Young Male's Marriage Primer

Power Tools for a Better Marriage

Cover Illustrator: Paul Forder pforde@fordesigns.ca

ISBN 978-1-60037-562-0

MORGAN · JAMES
THE ENTREPRENEURIAL PUBLISHER

Morgan James Publishing, LLC
1225 Franklin Ave., STE 325
Garden City, NY 11530-1693
Toll Free 800-485-4943
www.MorganJamesPublishing.com

In an effort to support local communities, raise awareness and funds, Morgan James Publishing donates one percent of all book sales for the life of each book to Habitat for Humanity. Get involved today, visit **www.HelpHabitatForHumanity.org.**

Dedicated to:

Helen. For your tireless effort, support, and sense of humor, without these this book would have not been possible.

Russell and Evelyn. I cannot imagine anyone having parents more loving, or gifted. I can think of no two people so obviously meant for each other.

Alison and Erin. I have been blessed with two outstanding daughters, each with their own distinctive personality, each giving me tremendous pride as a father.

Curriculum

The Young Male's Marriage Primer
Introduction

Danby M.D.

They call me the doctor. During the day, I'm just an average guy with a lucrative at-home woodworking business. By night, I become an amateur marriage doctor. My office, with most of my patients, is centrally located down at the local sports bar.

I wasn't always the doctor. Years ago, I witnessed a senseless tragedy at this very same bar. I watched a man as he laughed and joked with his friends—a ceremony celebrated by countless married males across the country, and a seemingly harmless activity. Even back then, I possessed an acute awareness of marital problems, and I could sense that he was struggling on the inside, struggling to find the cause and cure of his failing marriage. He struggled with the marriage demons night after night, sometimes till well past last call. Alas, it was in vain. His marriage failed through no fault of his own.

Let me stress that by no means was this an isolated case. I sadly observed many married males, each grappling with their own problems, night after night, week after week; never able to grasp the solutions they so desperately sought. I learned a sobering lesson from that experience. I learned that sheer effort is not enough. Total dedication is not enough. A man must possess the proper tools in order to succeed in his marriage.

I took a long, hard look at my own wonderful marriage. What had I been doing for all those many years (twenty-nine) that had brought so much joy to my wife? Why had my marriage flourished while others failed?

The answer was right in my workshop. The techniques that I applied to my woodworking were being carried over to my marriage, and with equal success. Each woodworking project I attempted required the proper tools. If I did not have them, I purchased them.

1

At some point, I had carried this philosophy over to my home life. For every difficult situation that arose in my marriage, I had developed the proper technique, or tool, to deal with it. Because I was so highly successful through the years, I decided to compile these tips into an instructional manual.

Thus, *The Young Male's Marriage Primer* was born. Life lessons learned from experience were transformed into manageable tools that the Young Male can utilize.

What makes *The Primer* better than the average marriage manual? Most, if not all, of your everyday expensive marriage courses are nothing but big textbooks with bigger words. The average married male tends to get lost in a sea of words they do not understand. You will not find big words in *The Young Male's Marriage Primer* (TYMMP). You will not find words such as accountability, and not because I don't know the meaning. (I could look it up.) No, I use everyday words, for everyday males, to be used everyday. I really can not stress this last point enough. Today, it seems like everyone is trying to break into this marriage-problem business and racing to come up with the latest catch phrase. We married men need concise, detailed direction, or lives can be altered, sometimes even shattered.

My wife recently told me that our marriage had growth issues. I needlessly went without potato chips for an entire week. This pain and suffering could have been avoided by using TYMMP's patented street-level language. I truly believe the text of this primer can be best described as easily understandable for the entirely confused.

Let me explain about my name and title. It is my name, but the letters directly following it can be somewhat confusing. When I first started *The Primer*, I noticed that most married males had one thing in common. They lacked confidence. In one of my earliest experiments, I legally changed my first and second names to Murray Dick, stuck the initials behind my last name, and then carefully noted the reaction. The response confirmed my initial prognosis. The average married male did indeed believe that I was a "Marriage Doctor" (M.D.) and his confidence level rose dramatically. Any feelings of deception that I might have had were quickly replaced by a secure feeling emoting from the married male, and the incredible gains that he was making. My clients call me Dr. Murray Dick, or M.D. for short; my friends call me Murray Dick, and my wife calls me something altogether different.

You may wonder about my qualifications. If you are talking about university courses, seminars, classes taken over the internet, or even owning a book of any kind, I have none. But if you are talking about a lifetime of woodworking experience, coupled with thirty-three years of wonderful, happy marriage and the mistakes I have made through these years, then you will have to agree that I may be a touch over-qualified.

The Young Male will be especially happy that I do not get hung up on grammar and spelling. These are of no particular importance to me and this allows me to concentrate on what is really important; that is, helping the young married males gain the prosperity that I enjoy. Besides, we are more apt to hear, "Dr. Murray Dick, your feet are especially smelly this week, I want a divorce," as opposed to, "Dr. Murray Dick, I'm leaving you—it's your grammar and sentencing."

I believe that every author has a style and mine happens to be flitting from subject to subject and then rambling on uncontrollably. I do these things very well and I do them consistently. Also, be advised that it is quite possible that someone may be using far too many run-on sentences, not because he is unaware of the rules governing this type of grammar, but because the period button on his old typewriter is completely worn out.

The entire philosophy of *The Primer* (TP) can be summed up in The Primer's Prime Objective:

The Primer's Prime Objective (TPPO)

The vast majority of professional marriage primers on the market today only ensure the total collapse of the married male. I do not believe in raising the bar too high, or putting the Young Male in a position where he is forced to achieve an unattainable goal. This can only lead to despair, depression, and negative growth. Instead of asking the Young Male (YM) to become a better person and husband, I like to focus on his miserable failings as a human being and gloss them over. Once the YM can look in the mirror and say, 'I'm pathetic, but that's okay,' his renewed positive energy can then be channeled in the direction of what is really important to a marriage, that being, the overseeing and stewardship of his wife's ability to adapt.

I briefly considered calling *The Primer* "Marriage for Stupids" after the well known self-help books, but I came to realize that average married men cannot help themselves, and they are more misunderstood than stupid. I have devoted much research time on the things you do and say, why you said and did them, how to cover up the things you said and did, and saying and doing things that you should never even consider doing or saying.

You will notice that once in a while I give the YM a break from the actual lessons and allow him to absorb the incredible amount of vital information. I have found that the young married male is slow to grasp and slower to retain as he progresses through his marriage. His attention span actually deteriorates to nothingness. In lieu of a lesson, I incorporate a piece of literature such as 'Agnes the Canada Goose' a truly inspirational epic journey of one of Canada's icons.

The Young Male's Marriage Primer is a survival guide to be sure, but it also shows the newlywed how to excel in his marriage. My easy-to-follow instructions cover the entire gamut of marriage, from helping around the house, to romancing the giggles out of her. Fulfilling the tasks outlined in the manual will allow the student to achieve Dreamboat Husband status and get his name on a plaque down at the local sports bar.

Although I focus on teaching the married male, it is not uncommon for me to address the young bride—either with her husband or off alone somewhere. I find it extremely important to convey to the young woman the reasons her husband acts the way he does. For example, when he comes home late from the local sports bar smelling of cheap beer and chicken wings, perhaps his soul is calling out for help. Perhaps he needs companionship and understanding, or perhaps he needs a large screen TV and a diet heavier on deep fried foods. I am positive that this type of marriage doctoring has never been applied, and once again, we witness the cutting-edge technology of *The Primer*.

The Young Male need not worry about coming forth with any so-called sensitive subjects and he will take solace in the fact that, although I am not a real doctor, I do honour the traditional doctor-patient confidentiality.

Take for instance, Milton Sweetzer. Milton approached me one day, and in the strictest of confidence, told me that he had quite a few pairs of women's shoes in his garage under lock and key—so many in fact that he was running out of room. I thought this to be a wonderful hobby and my solution was to share Milton's pastime with his lovely wife Ingrid, and perhaps help them grow together as a couple. I am both happy and proud to say that Milton now has the entire house for his shoe collection—at least until his wife returns from her extended visit with her sister. Successful solutions such as this one are common place in *The Primer*. It is interesting to note that all of the shoes in Milton's collection were size fourteen.

There are several people who I wish to thank. My father is perhaps my strongest influence, even today teaching me new things. He appears throughout *The Primer* in various lessons. Most importantly, he is the man who first taught me the value of a large collection of power tools, and how this can help in achieving the highest level of good husbandry.

My brother-in-law Wally could be considered a co-author; his input has been that important to the birth of *The Primer*. Although out of work for quite some time, Wally brings twenty years of master plumbing to the table and lately, he has been dabbling in psychiatry. He thinks that healing peoples' minds could be much more rewarding than repairing a leaking toilet, and with some experience, he may become good at it. Because of our closeness, I don't think it was much of a surprise when I asked Wally to write the forward to *The Primer*. He read it to the guys down at the local sports bar during the hockey game intermission, and most said it was touching, heartwarming, and just the right length for a forward.

A special thanks to my publisher Stan Frenway, a retired truant officer who owns Stan's Marriage Manual Publishing. I had no luck with any of the big companies—perhaps they felt that the state-of-the art, cutting-edge technology used in *The Primer* was ahead of its time. I thank Stan for stepping forward and volunteering his garage for my use. Then, in an unprecedented display of conviction and faith, he went out and rented a printer and stapler—with my own money.

I would also like to thank Gus Walmsly for marketing *The Primer*. Once it was published (all the pages stapled together), I was again met with resistance from the large marketing companies. Enter Gus, who owns Gus's Lumber and Marriage Manual Store. There, you will find *The Primer* on a display stand, right next to the plywood. Sales have been slow, so I had a book signing last week. Unfortunately, that one didn't sell either. Gus's gut feeling is that marriage manuals don't move this time of year. He feels that in a few months sales will be brisk.

The guys at the local sports bar have been very supportive, and are always there when I need them—right there at the local sports bar. A lot of my patented techniques and innovative methods were first tried on these crash-test dummies, and although some didn't work out very well, the raw data that I was able to obtain from these failures proved invaluable. They also voted me "husband of the week" once, and it means so much more when an honour such as this comes from your peers. *The Primer* will grow quickly if the acceptance of the guys is any indication, and as my clientele expands, I know that I can count on the patrons to become tutors. Don't worry about them being qualified to work on *The Primer*. Most of them think along the same lines as I do in regards to a strong marriage. I also plan on giving them a rigorous training regiment. They are already excited.

Finally, I wish to thank a loving, loyal woman who I have been happily married to for somewhere around thirty-one years, my present wife. I'm reminded of the old adage that I just recently made up: "Behind every successful amateur marriage doctor is an understanding wife—sometimes way behind." This is more than true in my case, and even though she has her own little career as a bank executive, or something along that line, she is always there when I need her. She has asked me to not identify her by name, no doubt to allow me to bask alone in the spotlight, and she has taken it one step further by legally assuming her maiden name. Not only is she a wonderfully unselfish mate, but she is also an accomplished speller. My wife has promised to help out in this regard when the second printing is published, if she has time.

Any doubts that I might have had concerning her devotion were put to rest when I asked her if she would leave me when *The Primer* became popular. Her loyal, but philosophical reply was, "Pigs will fly before that happens." I cherish this woman for her dedication, not only to me, but also to *The Primer*.

You have probably noticed that one of my patented teaching tools is the use of wise, old sayings that I make up from time to time. I have also been known to borrow them from famous individuals, altering them to fit the lesson. I like to think that Sir Winston Churchill would feel proud, knowing that he had helped a married man gain some sort of social skill.

Do not be surprised to hear a few quotes from my brother-in-law Wally. "The needs of the many outweigh the needs of the few," is one of his favourites and speaks of my unselfishness in going public with this invaluable self-help essay. "Beam me up Sparky" is another that Wally uses all the time, although he uses it out of text and it has little or no significance to this primer. I truly believe that Wally is wasting his talents in the plumbing trade, even if someone would actually hire him.

Let me say a few words concerning the extensiveness of *The Primer*. The young married male will take solace in knowing that the mistakes have already been made for him, if not in my own life, then down at the local sports bar. These have been analyzed, catalogued, and worked out in TYMMP. The student need not worry about future problems, *The Primer* is self-updating; I seem to be inventing new marital mistakes everyday.

This will not be a tutorial on real men. Notice how I mention such things as light beer, keeche, quish, quash (that fluffy little pie), helping out with light housekeeping duties such as dusting the remotes, taking out the garbage when you learn where it goes, and helping the wife start her lawn mower.

Let me be frank, *The Primer* will be emotional. The harsh realities of living with a woman will be laid bare, and any thoughts of excelling at marriage will take second place to gaining command of the basic survival techniques. The YM will find himself gripped by elation as I recount many wonderful, wonderful highlights from my highly successful thirty-six years of marriage. We must also be prepared for

7

tears. Many times when I'm counseling young people and I am relating the pain and agony that I have suffered (a lot of it physical), I find myself breaking into tears. I teach my students that it is quite alright for couples to cry, and that my wife does it quite a bit.

So there you have it Young Males, the outline for your great adventure into the world of successful marriage, a journey starting tomorrow with your first day of class. Rest easy tonight; rest easy in the knowledge that the trial and error has been done, leaving only cutting-edge, state-of-the-art lessons for you to grasp, learn, and finally try out on your wife. Lessons learned from someone who has been successfully married for thirty-eight delightful years.

As the lessons are learned and the tools are incorporated, let me issue a word of warning to the young student. *The Primer* is all powerful and must never be used as a weapon in the everyday living of our lives. Therefore, as a public service announcement, I am compelled to issue *The Young Male's Marriage Primer* Motto (TYMMPM) which every client must attempt to memorize and obey:

> *I shall endeavor to walk beside my wife. Not in front, not behind, but right up there beside her, irregardless of how successful, or popular I become. After carefully following the lessons taught by my mentor, Dr. Murray Dick, and implementing the tools I have been so unselfishly given, she will share my spotlight, right there beside me, not behind my rear, not up ahead of me, but right beside me. Of this I promise and I am not kidding.*

And finally, let me say a little something about the dedication of *The Primer* (TP) at the end of this introduction.

Years ago, I had a high school woodworking teacher named Ralphy Rutherford. Not only did he instill in me the proper use of power tools, and the value of keeping all of my fingers, but he wrote a book on woodworking. He dedicated this book to his wife who was his life-long friend, companion, and inspiration. This affected me deeply and I have never forgotten that. I'm sure that Mr. Rutherford, who has long since passed, would be proud to know that one of his best students had borrowed his dedication idea for his very-own publication.

I truly believe that becoming a good husband begins by becoming a giver. I know I have. Achieve this goal Young Males, and all my work will not have been in vain.

Thank You,
Dr. Murray Dick, (Danby, M.D.)

*The Young Male's Marriage Primer (TYMMP)
is dedicated to a woman who is an inspiration to
us all—Mrs. Martha June Rutherford.*

The Young Male's Marriage Primer
Forward

By Wally, the brother-in-law

Dr. Murray Dick is truly a visionary and he walks amongst us. A visionary is a man with the ability to see things—little things that are not there. Dr. Murray Dick sees these things. Not that he has bad eyesight. No, he has one reading eye and the other is used for distances, giving him the best of both worlds. He also hears little voices. But unlike many of us who also hear these little voices and sees these little things, the doctor responded. When he realized that he was hearing the plaintive, pitiful, mournful cries in the wilderness, and seeing the pathetic little faces of young married males in woeful need of help, he answered. He answered these cries with this wonderful, powerful work of art, simply known as *The Young Male's Marriage Primer*.

You have chosen *The Primer* because you have either bought the entire manual down at Gus's Lumber and Marriage Manual Store; you were given a free copy because you purchased some plywood, or because you were contacted shortly after your wedding announcement was published in the local paper. It matters little why, only that you have chosen the right road. Although this road will appear rocky, strewn with pitfalls, and seemingly senseless at times, take comfort in the fact that these problems have been encountered and dealt with many times by the author, a visionary who not only knows every marital problem known to man, but has lived them and survived graciously.

It is truly an honour to be selected to write this forward. Dr. Murray Dick had a vast number of candidates from which to choose down at the local sports bar. Milo Denny, for instance, knows many more words than anyone and even knows the rules to the popular scrabble game. Bert Toony, our local crossing guard who recently was forced into early retirement at the age of eighty-three, is one of the few who have any education outside our little town, having taken a few government funded courses in a correctional institute. Because he has been married and divorced four times, and also because his bail was recently revoked, I believe Dr. Murray Dick felt this would have imparted a slight negative impact on *The Primer*. He could have just as easily chosen Farley Drellhurst, our most successful entrepreneur, who runs a custom manure spreading operation in and around town.

Dr. Murray Dick chose me to write the inaugural chapter to launch *The Primer* and I suppose it is because we are so close (I've known him since we became related), and because we share the same vision. I hear the little voices as well and they have told me to continue my career as an out-of-work master plumber, but also to branch out and dabble in psychiatry; choosing a field I know all so well—the field of the abnormal. It has become my life's work in my spare time, and I thank the doctor for the inspiration.

In closing, let me say that there is something very special about this man they call "The Doctor." It is not the fact that he equates a large collection of power tools to a good marriage. It is not the fact that he is constantly improving himself. No, it is his ability to pass along the stark truth about marriage in the printed form and the Young Male will be all the better for it.

Thank you,
Wally, the brother-in-law

I just had another thought. I can only imagine the excitement that Dr. Murray Dick must have felt in his workshop when he developed *The Primer*. With his table saw droning and its blade rotating like "billy-oh," his thoughts would drift to matters much more important, matters that the average layman might find trivial and surely not found in any professional marriage primer. For instance, how to the gain the love and respect of your pets and your children with puppy dog bones and money, in that order. Also, a lie has a slight chance of getting you out of trouble, whereas telling the truth pretty well sells you down the river.

Thank you

Just one more thing, if I may. Let me end as I began. A visionary is alive in *The Primer*. He walks among us and we are better for it. Thank you, Dr. Murray Dick. Thank you for taking time out from your lucrative at-home woodworking business to develop, and share, your thoughtful insight into fine marriage doctoring. And many thanks for the good times, the bad times, the so-so times, and all the other times. We are humbled in your presence.

Wally

I am reminded of an old, wise saying that Dr. Murray Dick recently made up, "There is a fine line between a genius and the idiot in a small, rural town." The doctor walks that precarious line everyday for you, me, and all other married males who are fortunate enough to be reading this and I, for one, can never forget his unselfish effort. I wish the best of luck to all Young Males.

Wally, the brother-in-law

Just one last thing, I hope that I am given the honour of writing the epitaph on the gravestone of Dr. Murray Dick, should he be fortunate enough to die while he is still famous around here. There, scribed in granite, marble, plywood, particle chipboard, or whatever is handy, will be these few words:

Here lies a man, a mere man, a mortal man, but so much more than just a mere mortal man. He touched all those around him, not in a physical way, but mentally. From his modest beginnings as a lucrative at-home woodworker, he climbed the slippery slopes of life, advancing steadily, but never forgetting his humble roots and always having time for the little guy. Although he now lies in this deep grave, his spirit will forever stand high on some far away mountain top, or down at the local sports bar where he achieved his greatest success among those pathetic patrons. He reached the pinochle of success.

Never forgotten, missed often, always remembered,

Having a great time and we wish you were here.

Dr. Murray Dick, (Danby, M.D.)
1950 – to some future date when he dies.
RIP

Wally, the brother-in-law

The Young Male's Marriage Primer
Lesson One
What Is It?

Dr. Murray Dick

Before I could begin the arduous task of formulating the tools found here in *The Primer*, I had to discover, or invent, a definition of marriage to which the Young Male could relate. Marriage is tricky, deceptive, and fraught with hazards. Husbands are not equipped to do well in this kind of environment, and if they don't know the rules they haven't a hope of surviving.

I set out to discover a thesis covering the entire scope of marriage, and this proved to be no easy task. A fellow experimenter and noted scientist, Alan Einstein (I believe his name was), had spent the latter part of his life trying to find one single theory to describe the complete workings of the entire universe. He failed in his quest and as days stretched to weeks, I wondered if I was destined for the same fate as my well-known counterpart.

Failure has never been an option for this amateur marriage doctor, and I pressed on with a furious effort to find the single unified theory on marriage. I was doing some research one day, and as I surfed through the talk shows I happened upon a couple who were being questioned by a woman marriage doctor. To the untrained eye all appeared well, but I saw something that the average viewer was unable to grasp.

As the camera swung back and forth between the two participants, and the doctor droned on and on, the young bride was quickly entering what I call the "Cinderella Sector." With each passing remark, such as love, cherish, trust, and loyalty, she was settling more and more into her comfort zone. It was as if she was trying on shoes and rather liking the fit of each and every one. When the marriage expert got to the biggie, a lifetime of commitment, the bride had at last found her shoes and her beaming expression signaled the perfect fit.

During this same period, as the camera panned to the young groom, a different picture was emerging. With each passing comment, he was rapidly approaching what I call the "Deer-in-the-Headlights Syndrome." Paralysis, induced by fear of the unknown, was overtaking his young body and by the time the biggie came along—a lifetime of commitment—the only movement visible was that of his lower jaw, which was going up and down at a very rapid and unnatural rate.

Again, let me mention that very few lay-people were aware of what was happening here, and far less would understand the reaction of the groom. I understood it all too well. I wasn't always this comfortable in my role as a marvelous husband. Looking back on my own wedding, I remember being terrified when I recited those vows and it hit me. "Hey, this is 'til death do us part and not for a while, or 'til I get bored."

Let's face it, the average married male has a tough time committing himself to which TV sport to watch and what snack to accompany it. To him, a lifetime is either waiting for the second period to start, or next month's big power tool sale. The theory could contain no intimidating words such as dedication and commitment, but most of all, it had to suit the intellect of the married male. The theory had to be short; it had to be simple, and it could not contain any big words.

Using this premise, and calling upon my many years of trial and total failure, I was able to come up with something that all married men could comprehend and hopefully excel at:

The Single Unified Theory of Marriage (TSUTOM)

Marriage is nothing more than the Point System (PS). There are ***x*** *number of points in a marriage and the woman holds them all. The male earns points, collects points, and hopefully cashes them in. After this process, the points revert to the wife. The PS cycle starts anew.*

Finally, the average male had something he could grasp, learn, and implement. I was utterly exhausted from my efforts. However, I was also elated in realizing that I had actually been operating under the PS for years and had perfected its use. Who would believe that a talk show had provided the catalyst for this break-through event?

Before we begin the first lesson, let me say a few words about the Point System. There are many, many aspects of a marriage, and while some may not seem to be point related, do not kid yourself. The Young Males' days will be consumed by earning, collecting, and hopefully cashing in these life-giving points. Allow me to demonstrate how the PS works. I will be using one of *The Primer's* most powerful tools, my patented "Teaching by Example" (TBE) technique which follows:

The student may be wondering if he has ever met me, or passed me on the street. Perhaps you have. Think back to the couples you have seen walking hand in hand. I am the guy walking beside "THE MOST BEAUTIFUL WOMAN YOU HAVE EVER SEEN ON THE FACE OF THIS ENTIRE EARTH, AND I'M NOT KIDDING."

Okay, I have just scored one point here—probably more because I used capital letters and it may be read by strangers. Also, I want the apprentice to grasp how it was done. It was smooth, very natural, and it seemed to just ooze out of me. Under no circumstances can it be contrived, transparent, or artificial. A woman will see through a phony compliment easier than detecting a cheap designer knock-off.

By changing the wording, you can incorporate different subjects such as cooking, sewing, or cleaning the house. You are only limited by your imagination. However, use the tool sparingly and practice your delivery before attempting to score your first point.

I know what you are saying. "Boy! The marriage doctor is pretty good. He must have scored many points and cashed them in on numerous occasions." That is quite true. I have perfected the art of point-gathering, but there is a dark side to the PS. You can lose accumulated points before you are able to cash them in. How many ways are there to lose points, you may ask? I don't know, I seem to invent new ones every day.

The Young Male is now prepared to begin the first lesson. It is a tough one. I believe in starting my students in one of the most hostile environments known to the married male—taking the wife shopping. This is a situation where you can actually gain and lose points in the same time frame. The married male acquires points by taking the wife to stores and he loses points by complaining, whining, and whimpering every step of the way. We will cover all facets of shopping, from clothing to groceries.

I realize that some of the apprentices, who have recently become engaged, may be wondering how you can possibly lose points for an outing as pleasant as shopping with your sweetie. I am fully aware of the scenario. You and your fiancée have gone to the mall and have strolled leisurely along the wide aisles. You were holding hands and casually glancing in a store window here, a gift shop there, and you have stopped for something to eat at the food court. After an hour of bliss, you left the mall feeling refreshed, happy, all-giggly, and more in love than imaginable.

You haven't gone shopping. It's a clever ruse—a crafty female trick! Its sole purpose is to deceive the Young Male into thinking that his entire married career will be filled with incredible excursions such as this. These lovely outings are what I refer to as Pre-Marital Shopping (PMS). Young Males, I stand here before you and tell you that this is the only time in your adult life that PMS will be described as leisurely, enjoyable, and something you'll want to hold hands about. Above all, there won't be a whole lot of giggling involved.

Please be advised that the following is meant neither to scare nor intimidate. It is meant only to educate, inform, and hopefully help the Young Male survive.

Once you are married, that leisurely hour-stroll will turn into an all day ordeal of agony—with an hour spent in the very first women's clothing store you encounter. You will be forced to stand and watch as your wife attempts, and succeeds, in touching every article of clothing, at least twice. You will carry armloads of clothes to a change stall where she will disappear for hours and leave you alone with strange women who think that you are trying to hit on them.

You will finally leave that store and progress ten feet where the process starts all over. After eight hours in the mall, you have walked a grand total of twenty feet. At this point in the shopping marathon, your body starts to do strange things. You feel your legs tightening, your breathing becomes laboured, and you begin to feel a slight dizziness. You need to sit down. A glance over at the only chair in the entire store reveals two very large men trying to share it, and three more standing in line. Although mild at first, these symptoms become more acute as the day drags into evening.

Let me take a few moments to talk about this phenomenon that I have just described. Leading scientists have been unable to come up with any practical reasons why a married male's body reacts this way after spending vast amounts of time in women's clothing stores.

My brother-in-law Wally, an out-of-work master plumber who, as you know, likes to dabble in psychiatry, has discovered a theory where he likens this body reaction to that of a world-class marathon runner. After hours of pushing his body to the very limits of endurance, the athlete hits the wall. Wally feels that the average married male "hits the mall wall" (HMW) after a few hours of shopping with the wife. Wally continues in his brilliant summation to state that the average married female has an extra gene or chromosome, or maybe something else that allows her to shop for extended periods of time without fatigue. He feels very strongly that this extra thing was always there, but did not kick in until the invention of the shopping mall. In an evolutionary sort of way, it has allowed a woman's shopping endurance to evolve with the increasing size of modern women's stores.

I know that it is very complicated; even I have a tough time grasping Wally's state-of-the-art prognoses. His brilliant conclusion to the shopping fatigue problem is that The Himalayan guides, the Sherpas, would make ideal husbands, able to carry up to six-hundred pounds of women's clothing out of the mall without the benefit of oxygen canisters. He is truly a deep thinker and I only hope that he publishes his findings in an easy-to-read pamphlet in the near future.

Let's get back to hitting the mall wall. If you feel any or all of the symptoms listed earlier, please get to a food court immediately. You will lose points, but the impending results of ignoring the warning signs are catastrophic.

The end happens so suddenly. One minute you are standing beside your wife and the next minute you are going down, and going down hard. If you are a big man like me, you can take out two or three of those forty-percent-off racks in the free-fall. Everything is in slow motion; everything is surreal and so serene. You hardly feel the sting of the eighty-six plastic hangers as they slap and grab you. Then, you see a heavenly white light and a voice beckoning you to come closer. You are at peace.

However, the big white light is only the ceiling fluorescent fixture, and the soft serene voice that you hear is actually the saleslady yelling at you to get off her stuff. She is also trying to kick you awake. You are back in the women's clothing store and minus a lot of points.

It is a frightening, terrible picture that I paint Young Males, and there is no known cure for hitting the mall wall. You cannot hide. There are no safe havens in a modern day mall. Please do not think that you can find refuge in those spacious, well-maintained washrooms. You can only loiter there so long before someone calls security, and if you happen to live in a small town such as I do, this opens up a whole new set of problems.

Under no circumstances should you consider leaving the mall. That has been tried. I know of one married male who thought that it would be alright to visit a sports bar while his wife was in the shopping trance. He returned in a couple of hours, much happier, although somewhat wobblier, and he congratulated himself on his small victory.

However, the next time he took his wife shopping, she attached one of those house-arrest bracelets to his leg. When the felon crossed the threshold of the mall exit, the device was activated. A slight tingling began in the ankle area, traveled to the top of the leg, and then intensified into an explosion of paralyzing agony—an excruciating pain that lingered. I am sure that many a happy shopper entering the mall was surprised to see a large man writhing on the floor, desperately grabbing at his "groanal" area. The worst part was that most women didn't even slow down. He heard one lady say, "Careful Lois, looks like they installed some new kind of speed bump."

You would think that after thirty-seven-odd years of marriage, you would know your wife. Who knew that she was knowledgeable in electronics? I am hoping to make a full recovery.

Let's talk about those lovely garden benches strategically placed in front of fine quality clothing stores. You know the ones Young Males, the ones always unoccupied. They are empty for a reason that only an experienced, old married male like myself can explain. Let me illustrate.

Your wife is inside, touching all the clothes. You have just bought the latest edition of Power Tool Monthly and you have settled down to what you think will be a relaxing hour or two on this lovely comfortable bench. The key words here are relaxing and comfortable; words that have no meaning in a shopping outing for ladies clothes. Treat these two words (relaxing and comfortable) as symptoms far worse than those diagnosed in the hitting the mall wall syndrome. Young Males, I cannot stress this enough. If you feel the onslaught of either comfort or relaxation while sitting on that park bench, you must react immediately. Get to the food court quickly, or take your chances and go loiter in the washroom, but for heaven's sake, save yourself! What lies ahead is a fate much worse than collapsing through some clothing racks.

You are indeed sitting there reading and all is well. Then, you hear that little voice from within the store softly, and gently calling to you. "Oh honey, could you come here for a moment?"

You ignore it, continuing to read. This time the call is not so soft and far less gentle. Now you drop your head on your chest and pretend to be asleep. You even drool over yourself to make it look real, but she comes out of the store and with a light tug on the ear, leads you inside. You are about to participate in what all married men fear and try their utmost to avoid. It is time for the Dreaded Opinion (DO).

Visualize with me, if you will, Young Males. You are standing in front of your wife and a saleslady stands beside her. You are trembling, hoping that the question will not be asked. No such luck! Here it comes and you are cornered.

"Well, what do you think?" The question itself can be misleading. She did not mention anything about a new outfit, and I have been fooled before. Is she wearing the same stuff she arrived in? I pour back through my limited short-term memory and try to recall what her original outfit was, but I'm not sure. Should I press on and treat this set of clothes as new? I look over at the saleslady who is standing there with a little smirk on her face. There is no help here, not from a lady who has witnessed this comedy at least a hundred times already today. I know what the merchant is thinking. "Go ahead big boy, say something stupid." And you know you will. Oh yes, you will. You only hope that it will be less stupid than the last time.

You will say something like, "Gee dear, that blouse makes your ears look smaller." Or, your comment might be, "Those slacks make your hips look thinner, sure beats wearing those four or five pairs of control top pantyhose." Or, maybe you say, "Wow, that outfit is magic. Where did all your rolls go?"

I know what all you married males are thinking. How can anyone lose points for quality, heartwarming compliments such as these? And you are also thinking that this is as close to poetry that will ever emerge from the average married male's mouth.

You are correct on both counts. After discussing this problem with my brother-in-law Wally, he strongly believes, and I tend to agree, that something happens to a wonderful compliment after it leaves a man's mouth. The hearing receptors, located deep inside a married female's ear, change this comment in such a way that it is perceived differently. Wally feels that the average marriage male is indeed misunderstood—not stupid. He also feels that it is of no fault of his own, as proven by the ear receptors.

Wally and I continue to work on this mystery, but as of this writing, I have not been able to develop the necessary tools to eliminate the huge point loss suffered from the Dreaded Opinion. It should be avoided at all costs. In the meantime, if any Young Male finds himself confronted by the DO, I strongly advise that you walk over to the nearest forty-percent-off rack and just fall through it. You will actually be doing yourself a favor.

By no means is the horror of shopping limited to women's clothing. It extends to other stores as well. You have racked up some valuable points by taking your wife grocery shopping, and you are actually enjoying yourself in the aisles where there is little or no traffic. You are busy doing burnouts and wheelies with the cart, until the wife spoils it by dragging you over to the Kleenex tissue section.

This seems harmless. I will wager that most of the unmarried males buy tissues the way I used to. "Let's see, $1.49, that's pretty expensive. Oh, here's one at $1.29. Okay, we're getting there. AHA! $.69, there you go. We're done."

Since someone in their infinite wisdom (sarcasm) invented the pretty pictures on the box, tissue shopping has changed. Now, your wife parks the grocery cart right in front of the rather large display. She will then divide the cart into every living area in your house, and proceed to match the proper picture on the box to the appropriate room.

She begins. "Look dear, some lovely flowers for the kitchen, maybe a winter scene for the main bathroom. Oh, here's one that's perfect for our bedroom." She is going on and on, and you would like to help, but this involves some form of decorating taste and of this, you have little or no clue.

Suddenly, you sense the presence of shopping carts backing up behind you. You are afraid to turn around. You glance at your own shopping cart and see that your wife has worked her way to the far end of the house. There is still hope that you will escape this episode with no points lost. You begin to sweat.

Out of the blue, a head of lettuce rolls innocently by you on the floor. You now have to look back. What you see sends a ripple of fear through your body. The toughest looking grocery-shopping woman you have ever seen is standing there, slowly tossing a grapefruit up and down. She is purposely showing off all of her arm tattoos and, oh my, what big tattoos she has. Her demeanor is unmistakable. "Speed it up pretty boy or the grapefruit does what the head of lettuce did, only higher and harder."

I check out our "house" and we are almost there. But just when you think that it's over and you've earned those well deserved points, she says it, "And some pretty little duckies for your workshop."

You snap. You take one of your five-foot long arms and you wedge it behind as many tissue boxes as possible. With one fell swoop, you drag the entire lot into your lousy house. The excess boxes spill onto the floor, careening down the aisle where all shoppers, including tattoo lady, are heading for the exit in a dead run to save themselves from the maniac in aisle three.

You look at your wife and slowly, calmly, and with as much control as your trembling body can gather, you say, "You know that I love you dear, and I know I've just lost a great deal of points, but you are slowly … driving … me CRAZY!"

We will examine one last variation on shopping with the wife. That is, shopping for women's underwear. The average married male does not do this alone. We could, but our wives would just take it back. We would buy the stuff that catches our eye and also accentuates her figure—this stuff closely resembles the outfits we see on the all-girls' beach volleyball network. Our spouses would take that stuff back and buy what they feel is more comfortable—that stuff is sold by the yard.

You accompany your wife shopping for these underthings and once again, you pick up points. However, like every other event in a man's marriage, there are hazards that will crop up. First of all, lady's underwear shopping is a touchy subject. That is, you want to touch it, to feel it, even put it on your head, but this is totally improper if other people are watching. Remember, you are being viewed on surveillance cameras, and it is not necessarily for catching shoplifters, but more so to weed out the "touchers" that roam these aisles. If you recall, I live in a small town and trust me, being labeled an underwear toucher is worse than getting picked up for loitering in the mall washroom. You could, I suppose, wear a ski mask, but I have found them to be quite hot—especially in the summer. It is best to keep your hands in your pockets.

Another risk that will probably surprise you is the height difference between you and your wife. I am a tall man (well over six feet) and my wife is comparatively short. The problem arises when we get walking among the racks of goods, a silky forest, if you will. To some lady watching from afar, it appears that I am wandering around aimlessly in the lady's underwear section, all on my own. If this is not bad enough, once in a while she sees this large perverted person lean down and attempt to carry on a conversation with an invisible friend—or maybe a brassiere.

Eventually you spot this lady, and misunderstanding her reasons for staring, you put your hands straight in the air and walk around like this, showing that there is absolutely no touching going on. The lady now thinks that you have done something so terribly wrong that your conscience is forcing you to turn yourself in. Big men cannot win in the ladies underwear section.

Let me interject some personal thoughts on ladies underwear, especially about some of the things the manufacturers brag about. What is the big deal about an 18-hour bra? That's not so long; I once drove out west and back in the same pair of under shorts—a three week journey, highlighted by hot sticky weather on the prairies, and motel rooms with inadequate air conditioning.

These shorts held up remarkably well; well enough for me to contact the Fruit of the Toot Company to offer, not only my travel experience, but the actual underwear to be used in a commercial. I even sent them before and after pictures. They must be mulling it over because I have heard no response so far. The company may also be analyzing the photos for authenticity. I may, at a later date, send them the actual underwear.

One last thought on the 18-hour bra. Perhaps it does hold an edge over my traveling underwear. Thinking back on the conclusion of my trip, I didn't seem to have a whole lot of lifting and separating going on.

I guess I will have to settle for the wall of fame down at the local sports bar, where my underwear will hang with the other celebrity shorts. My brother-in-law Wally has a particularly impressive trophy. It's his coast-to-coast briefs. Wally undertook a grueling, five-week journey across our broad land in a pickup truck and yes, his underwear made it intact, all in one piece, sort of. It hangs in a glass trophy case to keep prying hands off, and to preserve what's left of its fragile condition. As unbelievable as it seems, they say that the shorts started off white, but the passing of time and life experiences have altered the colour to its present shade.

You know, Young Males, to gaze at Wally's shorts is to experience his epic journey. You almost feel like you are there beside him in the truck, sharing all the good times. You are with Wally for the annual bean festival in Thunder Bay, in Winnipeg for the all-you-can eat prairie chicken wing festival, and let's not forget the lobster feast with tons of melted butter on the Canadian East Coast As you continue to gaze, you also get a sense of the hardships of this trip; the grueling hours sitting in the truck, the time that Wally got the four-hour wedgie from the cowboys at the Stampede in Calgary, and the time that he got chased by a bear in Jasper, Alberta. I invite all Young Males to come on down to the local sports bar and revel in the glory of the wall of fame.

To end this lesson on the Point System (PS), let me reiterate that there is still much research to do on developing the proper tools to combat the marital problems that I have described. To deal with hitting the mall wall (HMW), I suggest you wear a light backpack stocked with various wilderness survival gear. Keep your fluids up by carrying bottled water, and don't forget those energy bars. I sometimes carry something to sit on—perhaps a folding lounge chair. Ask your wife to give you a week's notice before the shopping trip. Tell her that you enjoy fantasizing about upcoming events such as this, going so far as to call it shopping foreplay, thus creating an excitement beyond belief. In reality, you will use this time to schedule something else or plan a major illness.

For the Dreaded Opinion (DO), I can only offer you this. While there is no known antidote, be advised that Wally and I will continue to work diligently on this problem—sitting, pondering, and thinking, sometimes till last call.

And lastly, know this Young Males. You are not alone. I am out there with you and I am sure that you will recognize me. I will be the guy in the mall wearing the backpack, munching on a power bar, carrying the folding lounge chair, possibly clutching my "groanal" area, and walking beside "THE MOST BEAUTIFUL WOMAN YOU HAVE EVER SEEN ON THE FACE OF THIS ENTIRE EARTH, AND I'M NOT KIDDING."

Learn your lessons well Young Male.

The Young Male's Marriage Primer
Lesson Two
Communication

Dr. Murray Dick

Dear Dr. Murray Dick,

It seems that my wife and I don't talk much anymore. Actually, that's not entirely true, I think she's talking but I'm not listening. After sitting in on your motivational speech down at the local sports bar in reference to communication, I thought I'd give it a try and use some of your ground-breaking techniques. I waited until the intermission of the hockey game so I wouldn't be distracted, just like you said. I turned to her and said in a loving manner, 'You know honey, should it ever come down to it, I think I would take a bullet for you. In fact, I'm sure I would, maybe not in a vital organ or the head, but perhaps in the wrist or the foot. Yes, I would take a flesh wound for you or better yet, I would definitely take a near-miss. Yeah, that's what I'd take, a near-miss.'

She turned to me and lovingly said, 'If you don't smarten up, you may not have a choice.'

I'm not sure, but I think we've had a major breakthrough in our marriage.

Thanks again Dr. Murray Dick
Milton (not my real name)

Dear Milton, (not my real name)

Cherish these moments my friend. The avenues of communication are now open, and this small but necessary step that you have taken is the start of many more rewarding conversations in your extremely successful marriage. I'm already feeling the love. By the way, that was a great hockey game the other night, wasn't it?

Signed, Dr. Murray Dick

We go right from a most important topic (The Point System), to one of equal, or perhaps more significance, a lesson simply entitled Communication. I thought it appropriate to begin this key message with an actual question from my popular "Ask Dr. Murray Dick" segment which I hold from time to time down at the local sports bar. Milton (not my real name), refers to a speech that I gave pertaining to the art of conversing with the wife. I am proud to say that more than one patron came forward to reveal that they did not think that talking or listening in their marriage held any importance whatsoever. *The Primer* was built on the many marriage difficulties that I have witnessed at this fine establishment, and I thank these men for their many failures as husbands.

We have all heard it. Every married male has heard it—down through the eons of time. It probably started with a cave woman, who likely grunted out, "You never talk to me and I don't know what you are thinking. You never really open up to me. You never let me inside your thoughts, and I never know how you really feel."

The reply from the cave man on down to present day married man has been the same, "Ugh."

The women are right. We really do not communicate and it is not because we will not, it is because we cannot. The average married male is not programmed to convey or express his inner feelings. It's probably because he doesn't have any feelings on the inside. When your life revolves around power tools and TV sports, a man tends to remain a little shallow.

The Primer is here to help. By following basic, simple instructions, the Young Male will become adept, not only at conversing with his wife, but with using different forms of communication. Yes, we will be covering them all.

The basic Primer tool, Teaching by Example (TBE), will be used later as I guide the student through an actual communication that I had with my wife; a wonderful two-sided conversation that yielded tremendous results.

Let us begin by asking ourselves why we, as married males, do not talk or emote. The answer is that we haven't a clue. This is yet another area of marriage where the married male is totally confused and for good reason.

Years ago, when the Spaghetti Westerns were popular, my wife and I went to see every one of them. It didn't take me long to figure out that Clint was going to get in trouble with his female co-stars because he said little during the entire movie. I clearly remembered leaning over to my wife during one film and saying, "Honey, Clint isn't emoting."

She elbowed me and said, "Be quiet!"

Once again I was confused. My wife, with every other woman in the theatre, should have risen as one and yelled out, "Clint, you're never going to get a wife. You start sharing your inner feelings right now!" But no one did. They all seemed to be captivated by his inappropriate behaviour.

One older lady even stood up and yelled out, "Clint, come home with me. I'm willing to kick my husband Ernie out to the curb!"

Even back then, I was extremely sharp in the ways of marriage; the fundamentals of *The Primer* were already starting to form in my subconscious. Without knowing it, I developed my patented, ground-breaking marriage tool, The Primer Trial and Error Technique (TPTET).

I started my experiment by clamming up just like Clint. I would occasionally grunt, but for the most part, I remained silent. After getting nothing in the way of positive feedback from my wife, I stepped up my efforts by inserting various masculine phrases such as, "Thank you ma'am", "Much obliged ma'am", "You must be the new school marm, ma'am," and "Mighty fine vittles there ma'am."

This approach did garner a response from my wife who asked, "Is there something more wrong with you than usual?" I deduced that there must be another endearing quality in Clint, something I was overlooking. I continued with my experiment.

I started to wear a poncho around the house. It was an old one that Wally had found somewhere, and he claimed it was genuine Yak fur. He had put it away because in his words, "I just didn't look good in it." The poncho had obviously seen better days and it immediately started to shed hair. It didn't smell very good either, and I gained a much greater respect for Yak raisers, wherever they lived.

To complete the outfit, I went out and bought a cowboy hat. The only hat they had in our little rural town wasn't much like Clint's. Wally said that I bore a striking resemblance to Hoss on another western show. At any rate, I didn't wear it very long—it was too tight. When I took it off for dinner, the kids would giggle at me because it left a chafe ring across my forehead.

My wife said nothing of this until I came home one day with one of those dirty little cigars that Clint looked so good wearing in his mouth. This was too much and she said that, although there was probably some good reason I was doing this, it was time to cut it out and act as normal as possible. This was just as well because I was getting a sweat rash from the poncho.

Just as a side note, Wally did say I looked a lot like Clint. He added that I could probably be Clint's stunt double in any upcoming westerns. I had the same rugged good looks and we were both tough as nails. Clint could beat up four or five guys at a time, and I have gotten numerous slivers in my shop, running my lucrative, at-home woodworking business. Wally went on to point out that we both wore a poncho at various times. I replied that a career as a stunt-man was indeed tempting, but the family would miss me terribly. Also, horses of any size frighten me, and any kind of physical exertion tires me out quite quickly.

This entire episode left me confused, but I did come to a conclusion. While women look up to, and admire the strong, silent type, they prefer their husbands to be weak and yappy.

The next type of communication I would like to discuss is crying. This may sound strange, coming from a full-grown man who is also a Clint look-alike, but if the Young Male will bear with me, I will attempt to explain. Women seem to crave this type of sensitivity in a man. I believe it falls into the inner feelings category, although I am not sure why. Just to confound the issue, be advised that there are certain types of crying that do not impress women.

For instance, someone is working in their workshop and he picks up one of those slivers mentioned earlier. He goes running into the house with his "ouchie" and as soon as he sees his wife with that huge intimidating needle, he breaks down. He continues to blubber until she is done filleting his hand, and she gives him a, "There, that wasn't so bad. Wipe your nose."

No, we are not talking about crying from a serious, debilitating body injury, we are talking about emotional crying at the proper time. By proper time, I mean that a woman does not want to be sitting across from her husband at the breakfast table and watch him crying in his corn flakes, just because the kids ate all the fresh fruit. There is a time and a place for emotional crying, and once again, during the early part of my marriage, I was lucky enough to stumble upon the formula for successful weeping.

We had rented a movie one evening (it was a Beta and only the really old married men will remember those), and it was about a big farm dog. I wasn't the only man of my generation who was overcome with grief when Old Yellow got shot for some reason or another. The room was exceptionally quiet apart from the whimpering coming from my chair. My wife came over and put her arm around me in compassion, telling me that she had never loved me as much as that moment. If memory serves me correct, and it usually does regarding these moments, she was extremely compassionate later that evening.

Well, this event got me to thinking that maybe there is something to this emotional crying thing. I rented the movie about six more times that week, but my wife's compassion seemed to wane, even though I was darn near hysterical during the last showing. I had to move on and discover new venues for my crying.

Once again, I stumbled upon the answer by accident. We were watching a chick flick one night. (The word chick denotes a movie only a woman understands or likes.) I was actually reading the sports section when I happened to glance over and my wife was becoming emotional. Although not crying, she was looking sad and her eyes were tearing up. Sensing a repeat of our past compassionate night, I immediately burst into tears, wailing away for all I was worth. Unfortunately, something wasn't right. There was no big yellow dog dying in this show and my attempt at crying might have left something to be desired.

My wife asked me if I was having an asthma attack and wondered if I needed the inhaler. I casually replied that no, I wasn't having an attack; I was just experiencing a pretty large gas bubble. I now knew when to cry. I would watch my wife and emote with her. I just had to learn how to cry.

My answer to this problem was early Primer at its best. I eventually looked forward to these girlie movies and although I didn't really watch them or understand a bit of them, I learned to watch my wife inconspicuously and at the proper time, when she started to well up, I would spring into action.

I would reach in and rip a hair right out of my nose. Any man acquainted with this procedure will immediately agree that doing this will inflict a pain equaling, if not surpassing, that of childbirth. I learned this the hard way. One day, my wife reached over when I was driving and extracted a nasal hair that had been bothering her for a few hundred miles. The tears welled up until I lost control and I wept at the wheel. Luckily, I was able to maneuver the truck onto the shoulder before I passed out.

I know what you Young Males are saying, "But Dr. Murray Dick, I'm not old enough to have nose hair, or ear hair, or back hair, or any kind of gross body hair." My answer is this. Every man has hair in his nose; the younger you are, the deeper you have to dig.

Let us return to the lesson. As mentioned before, the problem is the severity of pain involved. The first few times that you pull out a hair, you are going to yell out in a very loud voice, "Holy crap! That hurt, my nose is bleeding, and I'm dying!" This exclamation will probably not fit into the plot of the ongoing chick movie, so you will need to exercise some sort of discipline to throttle your pain sensors. Some men are good at hiding pain, although I have yet to meet any. Most married men lose all control when the onslaught of pain occurs. We have to improvise.

For instance, my wife and I are watching a highly emotional girlie movie. My attention is split between the TV screen and my wife. Suddenly, I get the first clue that something is going to happen. The show's background music becomes quite full. It seems to be rising to a crescendo. It won't be long now. I quickly glance over at my wife, and yes, her lower lip is starting to vibrate. Her eyes are beginning to fill with tears, and she is reaching for her ample supply of tissues.

I wait for her barely audible whimper, and once this warning sound is heard, I swing into action. I brace myself and in one natural motion, I yank out a nose hair. I am immediately blinded by tears, but I have the presence of mind to blurt out my practiced, yet completely accepted response for the emotional drama unfolding on the screen. "Holy crap, but isn't this the most painfully disturbing thing that we have ever experienced in our entire lives? I believe that I am emotionally spent! Please pass the chick tissues dear." This procedure has worked remarkably well.

With some practice, the Young Male can achieve the success that I have gained over the years, and here is an added bonus. The more chick movies you watch, the less often she needs to reach over and yank when you're driving.

There is one word of caution I feel that I must pass along. Do not spend the entire first half of the movie fiddling with your nose hairs trying to find one that is the best candidate for removal. Your wife will spot this. She will allow it for awhile, and then pass over the chick tissues prematurely, for an entirely different reason.

Before we get to an actual two-sided conversation that I had with my wife, I want to talk about another manner that our spouses would like us to express ourselves—that being hugging and touching. On first glance, the married males are wondering why this is a big deal; they enjoy these activities and look forward to them.

I'm not talking about that kind of hugging and touching—the kind that is a means to an end. I'm talking about hugging and touching for no apparent reason and with no apparent finale. It is hugging and touching just for the sake of hugging and touching. Women say they get a warm, fuzzy feeling from random acts of hugging and touching. I have actually heard them say this very thing. This is not Primer humour. Not that we married men don't get that warm and fuzzy feeling every now and then. Often we do, but it usually means that we need a taxi ride home. My wife and I were on a walk one night, in early spring, and she said how romantic it was. It made her feel warm and fuzzy all over. I too, was caught up in the moment and I asked if she wanted me to call her a cab.

In reality, there is quite a bit of hugging going on down at the local sports bar. The wives of the patrons are always wondering how those greasy hand prints get on the back of their husbands' shirts. It's the old joke of chicken wing sauce on the hands and hugging your friends in a display of camaraderie, a bar joke that never seems to lose its side-splitting humour, and a bar joke that we married men never seem to catch onto.

I hope that I have not utterly confused the Young Male; sometimes my rambling style of writing does that to people. Do not be afraid to practice random hugging down at the local sports bar, and get in on the joke. It is truly funny and also surprisingly uplifting. When you feel that it is time to go home and give your wife a hug, make sure your hands are squeaky clean. Women have a weird sense of humour and they seldom appreciate this type of comedy.

Well, it's that time in the lecture where I present an actual conversation with my wife. Nothing teaches the married male like Teaching by Example (TBE), and I will set up the communiqué that took place over a year ago. There is one very important Primer Tool required here. Never go into a communication with your wife unprepared. Preparation, and I cannot stress this enough, is the key to this activity and the following conversation will show this quite adequately.

Another Primer technique that I like to use when dealing with a subject as difficult as communication is walking the student through the lesson. You will notice that I do not hesitate to stop the lecture and break down certain areas of importance. I dwell on these until the Young Male understands the theory behind the practice, or he nods his head in a believable fashion with his eyes open. I believe that we are ready to begin.

After months of careful preparation, I approached my wife with Phase One of The Communication. I began, "Honey, can I talk to you for a while about a problem?"

Okay, let's stop right here and analyze my opening dialogue. I believe that this opening statement marks the true genius of *The Primer*. With these few, simple words, I have gained not only her attention, but her elation and surprise.

First, I used the word "honey," a friendly salutation which signals that a wonderful conversation is about to begin. She feels warm inside, and already she is elated.

Next, I am asking her something; not telling her. Notice the use of the phrase, "can I?" She feels an element of surprise at this.

Moving along, you will see that I said, "for awhile." Now this is extremely critical to my communication in that I am willing to discuss something with her, not for a few short seconds, but for awhile. Be very careful when using these words, because to a wife, for awhile means that we are about to flog it to death.

The final word in my opening is very significant to her and this is, "problem." She is not surprised at this; she knows that I have a problem. In fact, she knows that I have multiple problems, so this is no news flash to her. But she is surprised, and very much elated that I am coming to her with a problem of my own free will. This never happens. She usually has to nag it out of me. I have approached her with something that requires no nagging whatsoever. She can save that nag for some other time.

Bear in mind also, that while wives do not necessarily want their husbands to have a problem, they also don't want their men showing signs of overjoyed happiness. Through experience, I have found that if you walk around the house all day with a big grin on your face, your wife is going to think that you have done something terribly wrong, somewhere else, with somebody else. Go easy on the grinning.

If you recall, my opening communication was, "Honey, can I talk to you for a while about a problem?" I am not at all surprised when she replies in a joyful tone, "Well of course you can my dear. You know you can always come to me with your problems."

I now enter the main body of our discourse, "We really need a new band saw." (A band saw is a vertical, wood cutting power tool.)

Once again, we will stop and break down this key piece of discussion.

Firstly, notice I used the word "we." I didn't say "I." We are going to go out and buy the band saw together. My wife is immediately thinking about a wonderful night out at the mall, strolling arm in arm, not stopping at any clothing stores, and happily entering the Tools 'R Us Store where we purchase our new power tool. We will then top it off with a lovely dinner for two at the food court, where I have secured reservations. This night out is commonly referred to as The Primer Dream Date.

The next word is "really." I use this to stress the communication just enough. We do not whine or beg, at least not at this point.

Moving along, we come to "need." This utterance could well be the crux of the entire communication. We really NEED. The Young Male should strike the word want from his already limited vocabulary. We never, ever, want something. We always need it or we will never, ever get it.

Allow me to interject a side note, if you will. I recently conducted a Primer Field Study down at my office (the local sports bar). This study consisted of me handing out cue cards to all my patients. Written on these cards was the proper way of ordering refreshments. The results were dramatic. It was so rewarding to hear all through the evening, "We really need a cold beer over here," or "We really need an order of chicken wings over here." I could not believe how fast these married males caught on to the concept of needing and not wanting, and I am proud to say that some of the sharper ones even went so far as to memorize the entire ordering process. Proof once again that *The Primer* will work if the student is diligent, hungry, and thirsty.

The last word we will be analyzing is, "new." We really need a new band saw. There was a lengthy thought process that went into selecting the word new, and this tends to get a little confusing. You see, we already have a band saw, but it isn't a new band saw, and I specifically said that we really needed a new band saw. But, if we get a new band saw, we will have two and did we really need to get a new one in the first place?

Whenever I get confused, or feel bad about having too many power tools, I just go to my wife's closet and start counting shoes.

Okay, let us repeat my opening communication, "We really need a new band saw."

My wife's response was, "Well, that's fine dear, you have a birthday coming up, and then we'll see."

Well, that wasn't very fine! My birthday was two whole weeks away, and anyone over the age of four knows that maybe means N-O, NO!

But I didn't say this. Her response had been anticipated, and I was well prepared to move on to Phase Two of The Communication.

I waited for a few days. I waited for a moment when my wife was relaxed and more receptive to my communication. I believe we were both reading the paper when I casually said to her, "Gee dear, I heard on the news the other day that some wonderful husband was making his appreciative wife a Christmas present when his beat-up old band saw flew apart. A big chunk hit him on the head and now the poor beggar's in a coma."

I call this my Primer Safety Net (PSN) for obvious reasons. No wife wants to see her husband get hurt, unless of course he has done something wrong, somewhere else, with someone else, and she's had a hand in the injury. If you do happen to get an injury, make sure you describe the pain in great detail. It is good practice in laying bare your soul, and your wife will love you all the more for it.

Alright, I've completed Phase Two of the Communication and the Young Male should go back and read it again because he's probably forgotten it.

My wife's reply to the newspaper article regarding the band saw injury was, "Well, it looks like the appreciative wife is going to have to wait for her wonderful husband to get out of his coma before she gets her Christmas present— right after the poor beggar's birthday."

I want to take the student back to the beginning of this exercise. If you recall, I stated most firmly that preparation was the key to successful communication with your wife. The most depressing part of this whole procedure is that it took me months to prepare my communication, and she came up with, and delivered her reply to Phase Two in less than three seconds. I seldom argue with my wife. I have studied this response for months now and I still don't get it. I think her response meant N-O, NO, because we haven't gone on a Primer Dream Date lately.

Most married men would admit defeat at this stage, but *The Young Male's Marriage Primer* was not built on failures. Once again, I waited for a few days before I initiated Phase Three of the Communication.

Be warned, Young Males, that Phase Three is not for the faint of heart. To succeed in my communication, I had to resort to a Primer Technique that required a strict discipline, previously unknown in my marriage.

If your wife is like mine, she is an extremely busy woman and to keep track of her demanding schedule, she uses a small pad of sticky notes. These are little reminders that she sticks everywhere—the fridge, the cupboards, and the writing board by the telephone. They are everywhere that is handy for her to view.

I take one of her note pads and write the words "band saw" on it. I then rip the single page off the pad and stick it on my forehead. Now, this technique will not work if you stay at home; but it will work if you take your wife shopping at the mall, go with her to visit her family, or better yet, go down to her workplace and meet her new boss.

By rigidly following the steps of Phase Three of the Communication, it will not be long before the Young Male is strolling through the mall, entering the Tools 'R Us Store, walking up to a salesperson and uttering the final statement of his highly successful communication. You point to your forehead and say, "We really need one of these."

Let me end this lesson with a word of caution. The tools and techniques presented here are to be used with the greatest respect. They are all-powerful and should never be overused. I suggest that the Young Male use these techniques in communications dealing with only the largest of power tools—those of 14 amps and over.

Lastly, we must remember this. No matter how proficient we become with our new dialogue skill, we should never use them to further our own personal gain. We, as married males, swore an oath when we started this wonderful marriage course. Our pledge is to walk beside our wives and to share our newfound success with them. We end with the condensed version of The Primer Motto:

To walk beside her, not ahead of her front, not behind her rear.
To walk beside her.

Sleep well tonight Young Males.

The Young Male's Marriage Primer
Lesson Three
That Unique Something

Dr. Murray Dick

Some years ago, when *The Primer* was still in its infancy, I was of course anxious to try out my new-found skills as an amateur marriage doctor. I would drive through town on the lookout for weddings, and one Saturday afternoon I was lucky enough to spot a group of happy people heading into a reception.

Just as a side note, by clever deduction I have been able to pinpoint the whereabouts of any new, potential clients; I listen for loud honking on weekends and watch for any cars with tin cans tied to their bumpers. Another clue, if you are on the ball, is any automobile decorated with toilet paper. The key here is the honking, tin cans and toilet paper; things you may not find in a funeral procession. Some people follow fire trucks, I follow wedding-reception vehicles.

After taking advantage of the valet parking, by telling the man that I was a really great uncle of the bride, I slipped into the reception and introduced myself. The ensuing conversation with the new couple was so uplifting that I decided to pull up a chair at the head-table for supper. I believe it was just after the toasts when the young bride leaned over to me and asked, "How do you do it, Dr. Murray Dick? How do you keep your wonderful marriage so obviously vibrant after thirty-four or thirty-eight years? Will you share your secret with my new husband and other less fortunate couples?"

Indeed I did. I talked well into the evening, telling her of the special something my wife and I shared, and how I planned to mold this idea into an easy-to-understand concept for all young couples. That was a special night for all of us. The results of my tireless efforts are here in this lesson—an invaluable Primer tool, "That Unique Something."

Our lecture today will be using basic Primer tools, the ever-popular Primer Case Study and later on, my patented Teaching by Example technique. This lesson requires the presence of both parties, and one thing you will notice is that I refer to the young couple as kids. This is another technique that I have pioneered and it allows the newly-weds to perceive me, as not only a highly skilled amateur marriage doctor, but also a wonderful, caring father figure.

The title of this lesson refers to anything that is special to a couple, something exclusive only to them, and strengthening their marital bonds. It is there for all times, both good and bad, and it will actually define them as a man and wife. For different couples, it is different things. Some may have a certain song, perhaps the one they danced to at their wedding; a song entrenched in their memory because of the wonderful significance of this ceremony. Personally speaking, my wife and I have never needed to call on that particular song for inspiration. We are truly blessed, but if need be, I'm sure I could find out what it was. I could ask around perhaps. Wally was our DJ, maybe he remembers.

Other couples enjoy each other's company in activities such as skiing or hiking. I know of one marriage where the two lovebirds are active in shopping and playing golf. She goes shopping and he plays golf. It seems to work and their marriage is all the stronger for it. And I am quite sure that there are a lucky few who watch T.V. sports together—indeed a few and indeed very lucky.

Let us begin our lesson with a case study that deals with a couple in their late seventies. John and Mary Doe (not their real names, professional courtesy), indicated that they were not happy in their marriage after I badgered them for a few months. I eventually hit upon the problem; they were lacking that unique something. I found it incredible that a marriage could survive for over fifty years without anything to bond them together. It is times like this that make me wish I had become an amateur marriage doctor years ago.

Through diligent hard work on my behalf, it was finally disclosed that Mary Doe had always wanted to take ballroom dance lessons. John Doe, a true married male, found this activity too structured, not risqué enough for his liking, and lacking in any kind of enjoyment. He actually didn't mind the dancing part, but he enjoyed the kind where he sat in a chair and there was a pole involved. He also stated that he did not mind if the dancers got a little muddy.

Calling on all my skills as an amateur marriage doctor, I proceeded to manufacture and implement a solution to suit both parties—a compromise, if you will. Let me tell you the truth kids, sometimes the answers are elusive and leaves me wondering why I chose this field as a part-time past-time. But "answering a challenge" is my middle name (not really), and the biggest challenge for me to date as an amateur marriage doctor was met and conquered.

You know kids, I have never been one to brag. In fact, most people find me humble to a fault. The results of this particular marriage doctoring were astounding, even by my high standards. As a marriage doctor, I cannot go into details (doctor/patient confidentiality), but I will tell you this. If you were to sneak over to Luther and Gertie Crumbly's house on any given Thursday night and peak into their living room window, you would see a wonderful, professionally-taught rendition of the YMCA song performed by the Crumblys—completely naked. And let me tell you, when old Gertie hits that Y-position and is perfectly silhouetted in the window, it can literally stop your heart.

And kids, with the careful learning and utilization of the tools presented in this Primer, you too can achieve the level of happiness that John and Mary Doe (not their real names, professional courtesy) so desperately sought, and with my help, achieved.

As I mentioned earlier, my wife and I do not have a special song or that special dance, and we certainly don't have that T.V. sports thing going, but we do have that unique something that has unified and supported us through thirty-six years of marriage. It defines us as a couple and qualifies quite nicely for my patented Teaching by Example technique. I shall proceed with the lesson.

There are very few details of my personal life that I will not share with a young married couple—such is my dedication to my chosen field of expertise. For a long time, I was unable to discuss a very sensitive event in our marriage. It meant so much to me, and I know my wife was moved—so deeply moved, that even to this very day she is unable to speak of it.

To begin kids, we have to go back, way back to when I was a young lad of six years of age. My father took me aside to give me that special talk that his father gave him, and he in turn gave me. I will give this message to my own sons, should I ever have any, and so on and so forth and the tradition lives on, as well it should.

He sat me down on a chair, looked me straight in the eye and said, "Son, you will never have enough wood clamps." (Wood clamp; a device used to hold two or more boards together while gluing.)

I replied with bewilderment and disappointment. "Gee Dad, I'm only six years old, and I don't know what a wood clamp is. Aren't we supposed to be talking about sex?"

But you know something kids, the man was absolutely right. Through all of my woodworking years, it always seemed that I never had enough wood clamps for any given project.

Oh he is a genius, my father. Not only in woodworking, but he is my mentor in the philosophy of life. He taught me to measure twice, cut once with your brand new band saw. He helped me with my personalized wedding vows, "With this ring I thee wed. Could've bought a table saw instead."

And now kids, I have a whole wall of wood clamps in my shop, and I have a darn strong marriage. But I don't have a darn strong marriage because I went out and bought all those wood clamps. No, I have a darn strong marriage because my wife and I went out and bought them together. That's right; each wood clamp represents a special outing or occasion, including some pink ones as Valentine's Day gifts.

The wood clamp became our unique something, although it was years into our marriage before I recognized the real significance of this basic hand tool. Kids, I must warn you that the following few paragraphs contain some of the most highly emotional moments in the entire Primer.

I was in my workshop one evening and I was in the process of gluing two pieces of wood together. I was just drawing the clamps tight when the revelation hit me. Suddenly, everything was so clear. The very essence of life, love, and marriage was right there on the bench in front of me. I had been doing this very procedure for years, yet I had not seen the true meaning. Had I been too caught up in my own busy life to see it? Had I been blinded by immaturity? I was overwhelmed by the simplistic beauty of the simple answer that lay before me regarding all the questions that I had ever asked concerning my marriage. I knew that I must share this wonderful event with my wife.

With tears of joy and fulfillment, I walked quickly into the house, not once thinking of my own personal safety. I dragged my wife back to the shop and when my breathing returned to normal, I began with shaking voice, "My dearest darling, look down there on the bench. Tell me what you see."

She glanced down and immediately replied. "That's easy, I see two pieces of wood and did you know that you have glue running all over the place?"

"No, No. Close your eyes. Look with your heart and soul. Search deep within yourself and tell me what you see."

She closed her eyes, thought for a moment and finally said, "Well I can't see anything now, but if you hand me a rag, I'm sure I can clean up that glue by feeling around."

"No, my little wood chip," I desperately cried. "That's us down there! We are the two boards; the clamps that are pulling us together represent our love and devotion; the glue is the strength of our love and devotion and will hold us together for a long time, getting stronger as the ages pass. These precious clamps, that represent the tie that binds, will hang on the wall when not in use, always ready, always willing to help anew, and like any well-constructed glue joint, our love will get stronger and harder as the eons go by, and no man will ever be able to tear us asunder or even pull us apart, after the wood glue sets, which represents our love!"

I was emotionally spent. Never in my twenty-six years of marriage had I poured out my feelings in my workshop like I did that day. I truly emptied my soul. My wife was equally overcome with emotion. She continued to stare down at the bench for a long period of time. Finally, she tried to speak, but she could not find the words to express the deep, passionate feelings that I had stirred. She turned and looked at me. It was a special look that I have seen quite a few times in our marriage; a special look reserved for only me, and first seen during our wedding vows. She slowly turned and went back into the house. I think she went there to cry.

I know what you young brides are saying. Sure, he tells us this incredibly romantic story but he doesn't tell us about the arguments or fights they get into.

Kids, I won't sit here and lie to you much longer. There have been bad times; times when we've had to pack up and go someplace special to regain our focus. One of those places has been Niagara Falls.

There is a big Tools 'R Us Store just down from the Falls, and here, amongst the power tools, we have hashed out our problems. She has ranted and raved while I fondled the more expensive tools until our differences were settled, or we were escorted out by security.

But you know kids, there are times when it is difficult for us; times when the romantic bond that my wife and I share with the wood clamp is stressed. For some unexplained reason, I have never seen a romantic greeting card with a wood clamp theme. It seems that the card companies have nothing for us at birthdays or anniversaries. My wife, bless her heart, will pick something off the rack. I think you kids know me well enough by now to realize that I could never settle for any old meaningless card, probably written by a machine.

Yes, I make my own cards. I would like to read to you the special one that I gave to my wife on our last anniversary. I never have any problem remembering our wedding day because it meant so much to me. It was very hot, so it was probably during one of the summer months. I'm thinking July or August, or maybe even early September or late June. (I do remember I was sweating like a pig.) It is these incredibly sensitive times that make *The Primer* so important. And who knows, if you learn the lessons and follow the guidelines, maybe you can pass on this knowledge to other couples in need of something precious to bind them together.

You know kids, I hope you find that unique something that draws you ever closer together. And hey, it doesn't have to be a big power tool, look at our something; a lowly old wood clamp. Your something could be a screw driver, or even a toilet plunger.

You know kids, I still get emotional when I think of that day, when I presented my very own anniversary card to my wife, and the effect it had on her. I was witness to love in its purest form that day. This I truly believe.

She opened the card and read it to herself. She continued to stare at it long after she was finished, undoubtedly trying to harness the emotion that was building within. She tried to say something but she could find no words. She turned to me and gave me that special look that I have come to know and love. She slowly got up and walked down to the bedroom.

<u>*My Dearest Darling*</u>
Our love will grow strong as our hearts beat as one,
In the cool spring rains and the warm summer sun.
But when our love fades in the cold winter freeze,
I'll just grab me a wood clamp and give you a squeeze.

I think she went down there to cry.

The Young Male's Marriage Primer
Lesson Four
Your Special Day

Dr. Murray Dick

An independent scientific study has shown that a woman displays a rosy, serene, radiant glow when she is expecting a child, or has just given her husband a brand new power tool. The degree of radiance is directly proportional to either how far along she is in her pregnancy, or the number of power tools given.
A leading pregnancy scientist, tops in his field.

One of the strengths of *The Primer* is its ability to bring raw, scientific data to the student. Today's lesson starts with factual, technical information from a scientist; and not just any scientist, but a leading pregnancy one who is obviously tops in his field. He probably has letters behind his name. Such is the makeup of *The Primer*, a cutting-edge, revolutionary marriage manual.

As we move through *The Primer* lessons, it becomes apparent that the Young Male can only digest so much at one time. It is easy to tell when his mind becomes saturated. His eyes become glassy, he begins to jerk his knee up and down, and he looks around for something to fiddle with. Actually, all married males respond in the same manner to learning, they react badly, but the Young Male stands a better chance of staying awake.

With this in mind, various methods were built into *The Primer* Curriculum to break up the monotony of training. Today's message incorporates one of these methods. A vast majority of this lecture deals with the young bride, giving the husband a much needed rest.

The first two chapters of *The Primer* were extremely important, but dealt solely with the young bridegroom's performance. However, Your Special Day might possibly be the single most essential lecture in this entire marriage manual because it involves the dedicated participation of both parties. The tools and techniques that I have developed and employed over the next few pages, if properly learned and administered, may very well hold the key to newly wedded bliss and ultimately, everlasting matrimonial happiness.

Once again, the lesson is entitled, Your Special Day, and I begin by addressing the young bride without her husband present, for reasons that will become apparent later on. My question to her is simple. "What is do you consider the most special day of your life, and does your husband agree?"

No matter how many times I ask this question, I always get the same answer. It is indeed universal. Their wedding anniversary is the most special day for all wives and apparently, according to women, their husbands as well. After a mild chuckle and a fatherly shake of my head, I kindly inform the young bride that, although this is a pretty decent day and well worth a mention, it isn't even close. She then begins rhyming off different celebrations; Valentine's Day, Mother's Day, Groundhog Day, her birthday, her mother's birthday, and so on.

Eventually, I interject and inform her that the most special day for both her and her husband is Christmas Day—more specifically Christmas morning. I explain to her that her husband is not attending this session because the mere mention of Christmas morn' sends a husband into delirious fits of joy. He starts to mumble incoherently, he will probably drool, and he gets to giggling. This reaction can only disrupt the class.

The universal phrase used by married males at this time of year is, "I hope I get what I wanted." If the young bride can grasp the significance and importance of her husband getting what he wanted, both their lives will become enriched in love and devotion. His life will be enriched for getting what he wanted and hers for seeing her husband so darn happy. It can be a building block for a strong, healthy marriage—lasting as long as there is a Christmas and as long as there is a giving woman in the relationship.

I have set the stage. Using two of my most powerful tools, The Primer Case Study (TPCS) and Teaching by Example (TBE), I offer two hypothetical situations for us to begin.

Let us look in on a typical married male on Christmas morning. We will call the man John Doe (not his real name, but we must respect the doctor-client relationship). John is awakened by his kids who are excited, as per tradition. He wanders down to the living room and sits down to await the opening of the presents. He wears the new pajamas that he was given two years earlier and the bathrobe he received from Santa last year. John is handed a present from his beaming wife. and he immediately senses how light the box is. He wonders to himself if he will be lucky enough to get a box of air this Christmas.

He carefully unwraps the gift, taking the time to fold the paper up neatly, and opens the box. With not a shred of enthusiasm, he says, "Look kids, Santa gave me some kind of soft shoes and they even have some fuzzy little balls on the back of them. What's that you say dear? They are called bedroom slippers and they match the bathrobe that I received last year perfectly? Gee, what a great Christmas present. I will surely cherish it forever. What's on TV?"

Now, let us retire to house number two. We will go to Dr. Murray Dick's house on Christmas morning. This is my ever-popular Teaching by Example technique, and one of my most effective marriage doctoring tools. It is six a.m. and we find the doctor sitting in his chair, waiting for the rest of his family to arise. He has been sitting there since three a.m., fidgeting impatiently. Finally, his wonderful family comes running down the hall, and he wonders why he didn't think of setting off the smoke detector earlier. As his loving wife and children gather around the tree, Dr. Murray Dick can contain his enthusiasm no longer. Disregarding the time honoured tradition of one of the children playing Santa Clause, he dives in, bulldozing the kids and the dog out of the way. Paying no attention to their whimpers of pain, he grabs the present that he has been eyeing for the last three hours. There is no need to check the name tag, it's his because it's big, and it's heavy, and it reeks of power. He drags it over to an open spot on the floor and rips the colourful wrapping paper off with his hands and teeth, singing Jingle Bells and drooling all the way.

"I hope I get what I wanted! I hope I get what I wanted!" His muffled cries are scaring the children, who are pleading with Mommy to put them back to bed.

And finally, it is there in his hands. He blurts out, "A Tools 'R Us 18 volt cordless drill, with battery pack, keyless chuck, and 18 point clutch. I got what I wanted! I got what I wanted!"

Dr. Murray Dick is excited. In fact, he becomes overly excited, and he starts to hyperventilate. His wife has to put a paper bag over his head to correct his breathing. Now, the poor man has to listen to his children open up their presents until his wife cuts two little eye-holes in his Christmas bag.

When I present these two stories to the young married females, I give them a choice as to which they would like to see; their husband wearing new bedroom slippers, or their husband with a bag over his head. Most of the ladies agree with the second choice.

Just a footnote on John Doe, and it is a sad one. I counseled John and his lovely wife Mary Doe, and I thought we were making good progress. But my keen sense of intuition, developed to the maximum since I started *The Primer*, told me that trouble loomed on the horizon. I even called my brother-in-law Wally for consultation. Wally, an out-of-work master plumber who, as you know, likes to dabble in psychiatry, conducted some preliminary tests but found nothing amiss with Mr. Doe. He even commented on what exquisite bedroom slippers he was wearing at the local sports bar.

Unfortunately, the very next Christmas, my spot-on diagnosis was born out. John got a lovely chartreuse turtleneck sweater from Santa, and I believe that this sent him over the edge. He was later convicted of trying to break into our local hardware store. An All Points Bulletin (APB) went out for a man wearing bedroom slippers with fuzzy little balls on them, pajamas, and matching chartreuse turtleneck sweater. A wonderful bathrobe completed the ensemble. Crime Stoppers got over thirty calls from the local sports bar alone, and we all decided to split the money and buy chicken wings.

John Doe needs our help more now than ever, and if you can find it in your heart to offer some support, drop into our local jail and ask for Melvin Cockleburs. I believe he lives in cell six. I know that he will appreciate the visit. He also enjoys the occasional oatmeal raison cookie, if you are really in a giving mood.

At this point, we end the wife's participation in the lesson, but it is important to note her reaction to all of this. To the average layman, she appears bewildered, confused, and her eyes have a crazed, frightened appearance. She frantically gazes here and there, not unlike a small pony caught in a fire, desperately seeking the nearest barn door. But to a highly trained amateur marriage doctor, her reaction is all too familiar and anticipated. The young bride has just been subjected to two of *The Primer*'s most powerful tools, and the onslaught of new thinking can indeed be overwhelming—even to a woman. Of course she looks confused, now her mind is swimming with gift ideas and things to make her man happy on their special day. Her "let-me-out-of-here" look is easily attributed to the fact that she now has the information, and the know-how, to save her marriage before it is too late. It is imperative that she get right to it. She is extremely happy on the inside.

I now bring in the Young Male and I briefly describe the topic of today's lesson. His reaction to the word Christmas is predictable and immediately he starts to jiggle and mutter. The mere mention of Christmas morning turns on the drool faucet. My client is giddy with glee when I tell him that I can help him get what he wanted, and also save his rapidly failing marriage.

I have his undivided attention, which is uncommon for even average married males, and I begin this segment of the lecture by asking how Christmas has been going in the past, and what has he been doing about it. The answer I get is fairly standard. "Christmas is so-so and not all that special. It's a time for giving, and Christmas is supposed to be for the kids," and other stuff like that. He also states that he has done nothing about it, but he is eager to learn.

Turning to *The Primer*'s powerful tools, I chose my patented, ever-popular Teaching by Example (TBE) technique, and relate how I can make Christmas into a wonderful, exciting, marriage-strengthening experience.

It's called communication. *The Primer* deals with this problem in another lesson, but I must touch on it to help the Young Male achieve his Yule-time goals. I continue on with the lesson.

I communicate my needs at Christmas by writing a letter to Santa Clause. I do this in late August, before the rush, and I post it in the local newspaper. I pay to have it read over the air at our small radio station, and I distribute my letter widely—wherever I think my wife will see it. Beauty parlors and malls are a good choice here. I also staple them on every hydro pole in a ten- mile radius.

In my dispatch to Santa, I just don't state that I have been a good boy. I list random acts of kindness that I would have done throughout the year, had I taken the time. I relate heart-warming stories about myself that are not easily traced. In short, I get the word out as quickly and as efficiently as possible.

As well as containing valuable good-boy information, I find it helpful to include my participation in worthy causes. One year at the radio station, I read my letter and with a trembling, emotional voice, I related to the audience how the Striped Bill Woodpecker was being forced from his habitat by an encroaching housing development. I vowed to fight this until my last breath, but I needed to make a protest sign. To construct my sign, I required a new air compressor and nail gun. The guys down at the local sports bar came through for me, and with their help, a new Save the Woodpecker sign now hangs in a tree beside the Striped Bill's sanctuary. This miracle would not have taken place without my new air compressor and nail gun.

The number of worthwhile causes is endless, restricted only by your imagination. One year, I sponsored a pod of humpback whales stranded on the shoreline of North Dakota. Last year it was my fight against the West Nile Virus, a disease spread by mosquitoes. I appealed to the public to help me purchase equipment for the capture, tagging, and electronic tracking of these insects. This would allow me to learn more about the mosquitoes' migration habits. Although I have never seen this apparatus, I am sure that it is extremely small and very expensive. Once again, the guys down at the local sports bar donated their beer and wing money for a whole day, and I am presently watching on-line auctions for some used equipment.

Let us move on. The Young Male must be creative. His return on the letter to Santa is directly proportional to the effort he puts into it. I like to include a tasteful little jingle every year such as:

Oh Santa you come down the chimney with ease,
Bringing your prizes which surely will please.
When it comes to my wish list I know that you care.
Please bring me some new tools, I promise to share.

At this point in the lesson, the Young Male usually asks whether it is worthwhile to visit Santa down at the local mall. I respond that it would not go over very well with the parents waiting in line with their kids, and appearing childish is never an option. I like to stand behind the white picket fence set up around Santa and yell at him. This works reasonably well and I can usually get halfway through my list before a couple of the bigger elves get involved and forcibly remove me.

The letter to Santa can take many forms. Sometimes it becomes necessary to take drastic measures to gain success on Christmas morning. *The Primer* has numerous resources if the age-old letter to Santa has no effect. In the past, I have written the letter on behalf of my father to his grandchildren, also known as my nieces and nephews. A quiet, but strong man, my father would probably approve if he ever found out, but I feel it best that he just sit back and receive his presents in the traditional manner.

I have always been close to my young nieces and nephews. In fact, they still call me Uncle Nice, and I do not mind that one bit. I cannot recall all the nice things that I have done for them, or even one thing for that matter, but I am sure they are numerous and heart-warming. Here is last year's letter that I sent to my relatives:

To those who dearly love Grandpa,

Well, it's that time of year again, the time when we begin to feel the Christmas Spirit. Our thoughts are on family and those we hold so dear. Perhaps we are thinking of spending a lot of money on presents for our children, our wives, or perhaps we are going to forego gifts altogether and just revel in the spirit, that is Christmas. I, for one, plan to shower my entire family with lavish gifts.

But that's enough kidding around. Let's take a short moment to ponder the true meaning of Christmas. Just recently, my Dad (your Grandpa) and I were holding our annual Christmas in the

Workshop and as customary, we were gathered around the table saw singing carols as we leafed through the Tools 'R Us catalogue. I believe that it was during our favorite carol, 'Deck the walls with lots of wood clamps,' that I noticed a certain look on his face—a look that portrayed his very own meaning of Christmas.

Although no words passed between us, I instantly recognized his train of thought. What Grandpa was trying to say, but could not find the words, was this; ' I could build so many woodworking projects for the needy, if only I had a brand new plunge router, on sale now at fine tool stores everywhere.'

I also believe that he was wondering if Uncle Nice (me) could find it in his heart to store this tool-of-good-hope in his own workshop, not for a few weeks or even months, but forever and ever.

Once again, we, as a family are faced with the $20 maximum on gifts. An amount set by someone, long ago, who did not understood the true joy of expensive giving, or the rate of present-day inflation. Let us remember that this is only a guideline and guidelines are made to be broken, or in this case, smashed. Here are a few wonderful suggestions. Maybe we can lower the set amount to $5 and pool the remainder for Grandpa's gift of dreams. Perhaps someone could forego their present this year, with the promise of an extra big gift next year. Perhaps an entire family could go without, as a sacrifice.

This man wears many names; Father, Father-in-law, Grandpa, and Great-Grandpa. With your help, we can add Grandpa Humanitarian.

To help everyone gain the spirit that Grandpa and I possess, I have composed a wonderful song, sung to the tune of 'Jingle Bells.'

'Plunge and rout
Plunge and rout
My good deed's done today.
Oh what fun it is to plunge and rout that wood away, hey!
Plunge and rout
Plunge and rout
I'm smiling as I play
Oh what fun it is to help the needy out today.'

We have two men with honourable dreams. One, to build things for the needy with his brand new plunge router, and the other, who is willing to store this tool in his workshop forever and ever. As you can see, we are doing the hard part. The easy part is left to the rest of the family. Please, I implore you; please find in your hearts, the compassion and love needed to cough up the money.

I beg you, the young children, the future of our family, I beg you to search your hearts, to search your souls, and to search aisle three down at the local Tools 'R Us. The giant display is about halfway down from the west entrance.

Let's make this the best Christmas yet. Let's do it for the needy and Grandpa. I will store it forever and ever.

Love, Uncle Nice

Although we failed to get the plunge router, I believe the letter had a profound effect on my entire family. All through the following year, I sensed a different attitude towards me and I felt that the entire family's feelings, regarding the holiday season, were changing. The very next December, I proposed to take a different approach. Still holding with the true meaning of Christmas but coming at it from another direction:

To those who dearly love Grandpa,

Can it be that time of year again? It seems like such a short time ago that I addressed Grandpa's grandchildren or grand-elves, as he likes to call you. But it is that time. It is Christmas, when we get that warm, fuzzy feeling from giving, or so I am told. Just the other day, Grandpa and I were warming ourselves around the wood stove in my workshop, reading selected passages from the Tools 'R Us catalogue and reflecting on the past year.

Although my father did not say it in words, I could sense that he was a little disappointed in his gifts from previous years. Yes, you little people are trying, but we really don't think that a battery operated nose hair trimmer can be classified as a power tool.

Luckily, I know Grandpa all too well. This year, instead of giving him something, I truly believe he wants his grand-elves to ask Santa for a power tool of their very own. Only then can they experience the true meaning of Christmas—the joy of plugging in and powering up.

Once you have acquired your new present, Grandpa would want to make sure it is safe for your personal use. That is where my kindness comes in. In an unprecedented show of unselfishness, I will offer up my workshop as Uncle Nice's Power Tool Safety Depot, where you can drop off your power tool, and Grandpa and I will perform the necessary tests on it.

Make no mistake about it. We will test it, re-test it, and test it again before releasing it for your own use. One of the most dangerous times in operating a power tool is the breaking-in period that can last anywhere from a few weeks to several decades. Grandpa and I are prepared to give up our entire social lives to break-in your power tool—no matter how long it takes.

So you best get busy writing your letters to Santa. Routers, power planers, cordless drills (18 volts and up), and table saws are all welcome at our safety depot. Although Christmas is about family, we will be happy to test any tools from your little friends as well. This is what caring people do. Remember, safety is a step in the right direction, and that direction is towards my workshop.

But wait, there's more. Let's say that you have been a little naughty this year, and you don't get what you wanted, or maybe you were just down right rotten. I am more than sure that Grandpa will buy you that treasured power tool and I will personally pick it up, free of charge, and eventually deliver it to you, completely tested and broken-in.

I think this could be Grandpa's greatest act of kindness in a long list of kindnesses; ensuring a safe and happy power tool Christmas for all his little grand-elves. I am already getting the warm, fuzzy feeling of giving, a feeling that I have heard so much about. Let's not disappoint your Grandpa again.

Merry Christmas,
As always, Love, Uncle Nice

As the Young Male can see, there are ingenious, creative ways to achieve your well-deserved happiness on Christmas morning. As with the entire Primer manual, these techniques are tried and tested. They are not guaranteed to work, but they will definitely get the attention of all family involved.

By this time in the lesson, the Young Male is utterly exhausted. He's been so hyped up from all the talk about presents and Christmas morning that he is entirely worn out, not unlike a small child coming down from a sugar high. *The Primer* does not deal with giving the wife gifts on Christmas morning, and this is not because it is unimportant. I believe a wife deserves a nice present now and again. I devote an entire chapter on buying gifts for women in the Valentine's Day lesson.

In closing, let me say this to the ladies. Great Christmas mornings do not just happen; they need to be orchestrated. Great marriages require the same care and total dedication. Get to know your husband. Read his letters to Santa, and more importantly, read his emotions. His happiness on this special day will reflect on you and your marriage. Your husband's joy should not be confined to an annual event; you must work on this aspect of matrimony, and not for a couple of years or a couple of decades, but forever and ever.

Good luck, Young Couples. Good luck on your quest for happiness.

The Young Male's Marriage Primer
Lesson Five
Agnes, the Canada Goose

Dr. Murray Dick

As promised in the introduction, *The Primer* takes a break from actual lessons every now and then, and allows the Young Male to catch his breath. We have just been involved in some very strenuous sessions, taxing the student to the limits of his attention span. I have plotted the learning curve of the young married male, and to even call it a curve is stretching things somewhat. It does fair better than the learning curve of the older married males, who sort of flat-line after years of happy matrimony.

It is with great pleasure that I take this opportunity to showcase my other great talent, writing literary classics. Today, I present a story of epic strength and heroism, "Agnes, the Canada Goose." A vast majority of my clients are unaware that, not only am I their doctor, but I am also an outstanding writer of prose. Come to think of it, a vast majority of my patients do not know what the word prose means.

The following essay is one that I have used from time to time as an example of dedication in marriage, the strength of the wedded bond, and allegiance to the family unit. If I could brag for a moment, I must admit that I am quite proud to be the author. My brother-in-law Wally, an out-of-work master plumber who, as you know, likes to dabble in psychiatry, perhaps puts it best. "Dr. Murray Dick, this story has The Digest written all over it, or maybe even The Geographic. It's that good. You should think of becoming a fulltime writer." Wally goes on to say that he knows of no other author who has mastered the run-on sentence like I have.

Perhaps Wally is right. However, we will never know because time constraints are working against me. With my lucrative, at-home woodworking business and my increasingly popular amateur marriage doctor thing doing well, I refuse to give up quality family time at the local sports bar to pursue another career, no matter how much raw, natural talent I have to offer. That was a run-on sentence, and truly, a fine one.

This story of Agnes goes back to a pleasant time for me. For a brief period, I wrote the goose column for our weekly newspaper, <u>The Marthaville Guardian Observer Clarion</u>. The column was entitled, *Take a Gander at Those Honkers.* So popular was this phrase that it began showing up as bumper stickers on local pickup trucks and was painted on the walls of schools and churches. The ever-popular saying appeared on my house from time to time, and for some unknown reason, it was plastered all over the local strip joint.

Unfortunately, a visiting feminist raised quite a fuss about the name for some reason or another. I was forced to change the title to *Honk If You're Canadian*, and the column ran successfully for two weeks. Regrettably, the feature was killed because of poor newspaper circulation. (They said they didn't sell a single paper the second week.) During that delightful period, I was paid by receiving a free paper, thus making me a professional writer for a short time. Both Wally and I believe that the professionalism mastered during these short weeks is quite evident in the penmanship shown in the following wildlife drama.

As with any literary piece of great value, I had to obtain permission from the editors to permit me to use Agnes in *The Primer.* The following is a release from <u>The Marthaville Guardian Observer Clarion:</u>

> *We, the editors of The Guardian Observer Clarion, do hereby give permission to Dr. Murray Dick, or whatever his name is, to use 'Agnes the Canada Goose' in his very own publication. The opinions expressed in the actual text are solely those of the author and not the editors. We take no responsibility for any negative feedback, and after reading this, you will undoubtedly understand why. Any ensuing litigation such as lawsuits, hurt feelings or hate-mail can be addressed to the author, Dr. Murray Dick. This goes for anything else he writes in this lifetime, the next lifetime, or anything he thinks, for that matter. This kind of stuff we don't mind sharing, you can have it. The Editors.*

With that out of the way and without further ado, I present today's literary classic. I dedicate this passage to all the brave Canada Geese who stay around our part of southern Canada for the entire winter, the locals.

Agnes, the Canada Goose

As the earth slipped by serenely below, Agnes beat her wings in the somewhat methodical, mechanical motion that she had inherited from her ancestors and past family members. Had it been five days already? The passage of time was indeed a blur to a wise, adult, female Canada goose on her yearly pilgrimage to winter in the southern parts of this vast continent.

Yes, only a few short days ago, on the quickly freezing tundra of North Toronto, she had felt the pangs of change reverberate through her large goose-feathered body. The leader of the pack, Murray Dick rose and uttered his yearly summons, "Honk, Honk, Honkity Honk." (Arise my fellow flockers, the winds of change blow freely, the time is nigh to follow the seasons, and please arrange yourselves in an orderly V-formation.) She knew then that her instincts had not failed her.

And now, as the barren fields passed below, she marveled at Murray Dick's intuition. The signs of approaching winter were everywhere. Small Inuit boys of North Toronto were preparing hockey rinks in their backyards and indeed, while flying low one day, some of the younger members of the flock narrowly missed being hit right in the beak by a wayward slap shot. She witnessed ever increasing numbers of snowmobiles being prepared for winter-frolicking by young, delinquent lads. A growing restlessness inside her warned that this would be a long and hard winter for those left behind and also for those staying. Confirming this feeling was the fact that she could see housewives splitting vast quantities of firewood.

Glancing at the front of the V, Agnes could not help but look at Murray Dick, as fine a goose as ever was produced in the Canadian North. As leader, he had taken the point for the majority of their flight, and the agonizing torture and billowing of the wind had developed his muscles much more than the other males. He was very buff and as her thoughts wandered to things she should not be thinking, she glanced over at her own mate Wally, who was struggling near the back of the formation—not so muscular, and indeed, far from buff. Wally's expertise was finding food on the frozen tundra and then consuming every last chunk of it. While this was a trait that ensured the survival of many creatures in the wild, Wally would never have to worry about fading away.

As her gaze went back to that big, strong, hunk-of-a-goose Murray Dick, she found herself thinking of things that could have been, things that should have been, things that would have been, and many other things that could, should, and would have been. Silently, she cursed the fate of the Canada goose. She, like all other members of Canada Goosedom, had mated for life. Oh, woe was she, but it would not be her that destroyed this time-honoured tradition.

One day, while cruising low, the flock passed a pair of loons, also migrating south. This stirred an emotion in Agnes that surfaced whenever she encountered these equally majestic birds. Why had the Canadian government selected the loon to grace its new one-dollar coin? Had not her ancestors worn the proud Canadian name for millennia and maybe longer, and suffered so much more in their journeys? Would the people of the Great North not have been more proud with the goosy instead of the loony?

Her pangs of regret were replaced with thoughts of the journey at hand as the handsome loons rapidly fell aback. They were much slower flyers, probably because they were known throughout the fowl kingdom as bottom heavy. Truth-be-told, they couldn't fly ten feet above the ground to save their lives, and she wasn't sure about their mating system, if they indeed had one. Hadn't she heard stories about them sleeping around the pond? Sure, they could hold their breath underwater for about four days, but that's not helping them a lot up here, now is it? She quickly dismissed these thoughts before they became petty.

On and on she flew, working her way to the front to take her turn breaking the wind, and watching as her mate managed to stay at the rear. Wally's excuses were legendary; a sore wing here, a severe pain in his beak there, "I'm kind of tired this morning," or "I must have gotten into some bad corn last night." There was always something to keep him riding in the calm. But this mattered little to Agnes; she would continue to honour her family's name with continuous treks to the front and to Murray Dick—the goose with the body to die for.

She flew with confidence and contentment, feeling safe and secure in the knowledge that below them, the Canadian Decoy Registry had completely eliminated hunting crimes. The litigated registering of all decoys had ensured the safe passage of millions of ducks, geese, and other waterfowl through this fair and liberal country. On another note, but of no less importance, the Registry had prohibited the use of fat decoys that tended to confuse the slower geese. In past years, it seemed that Wally was always pointing his wing to one of these so called well-fed deceptions and asking Murray Dick if they could pull over for a quick bite.

At night, Agnes rested in familiar fields, safe havens remembered from years past, and after grazing on the succulent harvest of various grains and other fodder, she would fall off to sleep. It was a restless sleep, punctuated with dreams of the dangers that lie ahead, and occasional thoughts of Murray Dick, that majestic, "hunka, hunka, burnin' goose." The morning would find her stirring, along with thousands of still weary travellers throwing off the dregs of sleep, knowing that they must go on, could go on, and should go on. It was Murray Dick, of course, the leader of the pack who took charge as always, and that big, strong, sleek specimen would rally the troops, "Honk!!! Honk!!! Honkity Honk!!" (We must reassemble, we must continue our journey, women and children to the rear, and would someone please go and get Wally out of the cornfield.)

Of her own two offspring, Agnes was both proud and disappointed. Her daughter Trudy showed all the signs of maturing into a wonderful adult goose, adept at finding food for her and her mate, and also flying with a strength that belied her young age. Her son Billy was a different matter, constantly in trouble for flying in the middle of the V, hitching a ride by clamping his beak around tail feathers in front of him, and for flirting with the young females during flight. Wally was always dropping back to discipline Billy. Actually, he would instruct the young lad on the proper way to flirt while in flight, and how to secure the easiest ride on someone's tail feathers. The spirit of his father grew strong in young Billy.

As the days turned into weeks, and the weeks into months, a sense of uneasiness gripped Agnes. Perhaps it was goose intuition, perhaps it was millions of years of innate knowledge, or perhaps it was the backup of trailers and motor homes at a familiar checkpoint below. Whatever the reason, Agnes knew that they were approaching the American border, and every senior Canadian, who still had a driver's license, was heading south. She hoped that they had all purchased special snow bird health insurance in case of out-of-country medical needs.

Once again, it was Murray Dick, that wise and cagey leader of the pack who took charge, "Honk!! Honk!! Honkity Honk!! "(Be advised that we are leaving Canada and the protection of the Decoy Registry and entering the United States of America and their "pry my decoy from my cold, dead hands" policy. Beware of hunters possessing a concealed decoy permit, and Wally, stop biting that female goose on the tail feathers.)

Luckily, Agnes' trip to the Chesapeake Bay is uneventful. The Native-American meaning of this great body of water is "shell fish." Today's version is "great big sea where obnoxious personal watercraft abound." Fortunately, these boats come with a built-in warning device and there is seldom any need for Murray Dick to alert the flock. They would never hear him anyway.

The winter is spent in the beauty of the great bay. Agnes, content with the bounty offered in this haven, watches her family with knowing, loving eyes. Her daughter Trudy was gaining strength and maturity with the passing of each day. Billy was gaining confidence, but still retained that impish, rascal quality. He seemed to spend lots of time in the bad-goose corner of the pond. Her mate Wally, ever the gatherer, but more so the eater spends his time showing the younger geese how to waddle their way through the all-you-can-eat corn field buffet.

The Chesapeake Bay winter is kind to Agnes and her family, alas to all of the flock in its entirety. The mild, not-quite-freezing days, give her a chance to extend her home, flying to far off reaches of the bay and its multitudes of estuaries and creeks. Very few of the adult geese are allowed to lead forays into new territories because of local hunters and their concealed-carry decoy permits, but Murray Dick has shown complete trust in her leadership. This new kinship spurs her on to a fresh series of adult dreams of her and Murray Dick, that muscle-bound, rock-hard, meaty, stud-of-a-goose. But alas, the moral plight of mating for life keeps both her webbed feet planted firmly on the ground.

All too soon, the cycle will begin anew. There will be a stirring in the soul of Agnes, a feeling of uneasiness, and each goose will once again respond to the unquenchable demand that radiates from deep within his or her soul. As always, it is Murray Dick who spurs the flock to action. "Honk!! Honk!! Honkity Honk!!"(Okay folks, it's that time again. You kids are older and stronger than last fall, so you get in behind me. Women, as always, start at the back and work your way up to the front. Billy, put the young female down, don't make me come over there, and Wally, I'll not tell you again, you've never been much good at flying with a corncob in your beak!)

The End

Well, there you have it Young Males—an epic story of a magnificent fowl that I have not only admired, but eaten for years. The Canada goose is truly a Canadian icon. Not only is the tale entertaining, but Wally, ever the dabbler in psychiatry, believes there is quite a bit of philosophical meaning hidden deep within the story. This will undoubtedly be incorporated into *The Primer* as soon as we figure out what it is. He also says that there may be some irony in the story as well and how lucky is that?

Wally goes on to point out that the story might flow better if the names of the geese are switched around somewhat. I think the names, as they stand, lend credibility to the epic saga of survival and whatever else anybody would like to read into the story. I did hear that there was irony in there somewhere.

We have much work to do in future chapters, but I feel that breaks in teaching refresh the Young Male's mind, and he will be better able to absorb the remaining lessons with a clear, empty head. With this in mind, we will push on to the next lesson.

The Young Male's Marriage Primer
Lesson Six
Nocturnal Habits of the Married Male

Dr. Murray Dick

The Young Male will undergo several lifestyle changes once he is married. For one, he won't be cruising the lumberyard for chicks anymore, and more importantly, he will not be sleeping by himself as often as when he was single. This new sleeping arrangement can be a tremendous source of enjoyment for him, and also a well-deserved form of amusement for his wife.

Unfortunately, there are a few drawbacks to this idyllic setting. He will be accused of doing things in bed which will put a strain on his marriage. Those things are snoring, unnecessary talking while asleep, and unwanted movements in bed. Simply labeled, these are "The Nocturnal Habits of the Married Male."

It should be apparent by now that *The Young Male's Marriage Primer* addresses all important marriage trouble areas head-on. In this lesson, we will look extensively at these night-time issues. If you recall, back in the introduction, we discussed The Primer Prime Objective (TPPO). Let me paraphrase this most important message. *"Any faults of the married male that we cannot fix, we shall gloss over. We then concentrate on what is really important in the development of a successful marriage; working on your wife's ability to adapt."*

What this means is that I have failed in my attempts to cure the married male of these unwanted nocturnal habits. Yes, I have fallen short, but not from lack of effort.

Even as we speak, my brother-in-law Wally and I are conducting extensive research down at the local sports bar. We conducted a Primer Poll (PP) among the patrons asking them if they snored. The results were staggering. Not one of the married males snored. We also gathered this startling scientific data; most wives were chronic complainers.

This ground-breaking evidence would have been enough for most amateur marriage doctors, but I needed more proof that married men do not snore. I sent Wally on a Primer Field Study (PFS) and the outcome was astonishing. He was able to peak into more than a dozen bedroom windows before being arrested, and he concluded that there are two types of married males; those who snore and those who are big, fat liars. Wally did say that a few of the males may not have been snoring per se, but could have been trying to snort up small pieces of food in their sleep. This is a safety mechanism that the married male has developed after years of eating chicken wings, and then going directly to bed. It is actually quite normal.

I then looked back at my highly successful marriage and realized that for a goodly number of years, I was in the denial camp. "If I was snoring and it was that bad, why didn't I didn't wake myself up?" or "It's probably the dog snoring at night." My wedding vows said something about, "to have and to fold, in richness and in death," and other stuff like that. Nowhere did it say that I had to believe everything bad that my wife had to say about me.

The first small hint that she may have been telling the truth was when the kids told me that I snored—the kids across the street. Apparently, I was loud also. Sensing that I was now "awakened," my wife preceded to tell me one of the most fascinating stories that I have ever heard regarding nocturnal behaviour.

It seems that during the many years of our marriage, I had progressed through the norm of ordinary snoring until it had taken on a distinctiveness all its own. According to my wife, I didn't just snore; I uttered many different noises. She has been able to identify 283 different sounds and categorize them in a file on our night stand. They come out of my mouth and also my nasal passages, in no structured order, and without any warning.

The first sound on the list is what my wife calls 'the biggie,' or the "big boat in the fog." This one is unsurpassed in volume and the ability to disturb the neighbourhood sleep patterns. After all these years, she still feels a sense of panic when the big boat erupts. She claims it even vibrates her sternum (wherever that is), which I would have thought was a good thing.

My wife also related that on some nights, she actually felt peaceful with my many sounds. Often, she could picture herself in a zoo with many cat-like animals purring and softly growling under their breath; or she is in a farm setting with many large barnyard animals chewing on food, burping and making gurgling, digestive noises. Other nights, she would imagine being at Sea World, with my rendition so real; she could imagine herself lying next to an elephant seal.

She has spent many serene, peaceful nights resting in a garden with the hum of insects, the call of the tree frogs, and the tweeting of song birds. How lovely it was when a small delicate hummingbird appeared with its wings droning, flitting here and there across the bedroom, spreading a sense of calmness and tranquility.

But just as my wife became enveloped in the serenity of the moment, the big boat in the fog would show up and there goes her sternum again, vibrating along with the bedroom furniture and the entire contents of the bathroom medicine cabinet. The dog would bark, car alarms would go off around the neighbourhood, and the kids' ongoing nightmares about Armageddon would commence.

Well, it didn't sound too bad to me. I am a firm believer in the old saying regarding "if it ain't broke." However, the Young Males also know that I hold perfection pretty dearly in my home life, and I set about to repair this slight problem in my incredibly successful marriage.

I called upon Thomas Cringe, our resident inventor. Thomas is somewhere around eighty-five years of age and lives down at the local trailer park. I explained my dilemma to Thomas and asked him if he could come up with a device to help me overcome this minor difficulty. He conducted some tests on me—one dealt with me lying down in his trailer while he sat in a chair, staring at me and making notes while I slept. I found out that I have trouble falling asleep while a man is looking at me, although Old Tom didn't seem to mind. He fell asleep almost immediately and after listening to his snoring problem, I woke him up and asked him if this was part of the test. Thomas couldn't remember any test, so he said that we should move on to the next phase.

I was told to lie down while Tom held my nostrils shut tight. After telling me to breathe as normally as possible, he put his face down really close to mine. He then started yelling loudly into my mouth and listening. I asked Thomas if there was a chance this experiment might possibly get even weirder than it was at this instance. He replied that he was checking my oral cavity for echo. He could not begin to construct something to combat my snoring without proper resonance readings of my mouth.

Thomas did indeed get his results, but I found the experiment rather unnerving. There is something unsettling, even by my standards, about having your nostrils held shut while an older man yells directly into your wide open mouth. You stare up at this individual hovering directly over your face and strangely enough, your thoughts go to those denture adhesive commercials, and you hope that they are telling the truth.

It wasn't too many days later that Thomas Cringe was knocking at my door with his latest invention; The Cringe Anti-Snore Device. It was a strange looking thing, made up of a very heavy rubber strap that could be tightened, or loosened, depending on the size of the wearer's skull. Two rather large plastic hooks were attached to the front of the strap. The hooks, or fingers, were specially shaped to fit inside the nostrils and when the rubber band was pulled taut, the hooks opened the nostrils.

Old Tom said it was very comfortable. Obviously, old Tom never wore the thing. First of all, the big rubber band made it extremely heavy. My head immediately fell to one side when I put it on, but I figured this was alright. If I couldn't crawl wearing this thing while awake, I wouldn't be doing a whole lot of walking in my sleep.

Attaching the device to my head turned out to be a two-man operation. Night time would find my wife directly behind me, ready to spring into action as soon as I had the nostril fingers placed properly. When I gave the word, she would pull the rubber bands tight, which in turn, would pry my nostrils open. Keep in mind that my wife usually does not pay much attention to my friends' inventions, but this was different. This could mean a good night's sleep for her. Consequently, she was all too happy to help. She also caught on to the fact that, the tighter the device, the more open the nostrils—possibly resulting in less snoring. She would then sink her knee into my back, and with both hands, she would give a mighty heave-ho on the rubber bands. My nostrils would immediately fly open to the point where I was unable to close my eyes. My wife called this operation, "cinching the saddle."

It is funny, but this device did work. Oh sure, the kids made fun of Daddy's automatic nose-picker, but it did stop me from snoring. There was one drawback however. After my wife finished cinching me, the device turned into a head tourniquet, and I lost all feeling in the upper part of my skull. One night, my wife got some of her friends to help her adjust the device, and they obviously overdid it. Unbeknownst to anyone, it began working its way to the top of my head, and at about 2:30 a.m.., the "Cringe" shot off the top of my skull, ricocheted off the headboard, and blew a hole in my wife's dresser mirror.

This had quite an effect on my wife. She enjoyed the restful nights, but she realized she was sleeping beside a loaded weapon. She said that she kept waking up, afraid that my head was aiming at her. I was told to sleep in the opposite direction of her, with my feet on the pillow, but I complained about feeling suffocated with my head down under the covers. My wife responded that with my feet in her general vicinity, it was no picnic for her either. We both decided, in the interest of safety, to return the "Cringe" to Thomas for some fine tuning.

When I went back to the trailer camp, Thomas said he was not at all surprised in seeing me. He realized that the design was faulty, and sooner or later, something terrible would happen—either a small child would get hit by the device or my nostrils would get ripped from my face. I asked him if maybe he should have informed me about these little flaws before I had the bad experiences. He said he would have told me, but he had forgotten who he had given the apparatus to. He had been on the lookout for someone around town with stretched nostrils and rubber band marks around his head.

Although the Cringe Anti-Snore Device did not make it to production, I believe it was the inspiration for today's nose strips that hold the nostrils open from the outside, using sticky tape. The Cringe did outweigh the new strips by about forty pounds, and I've since used the heavy rubber bands to anchor camping equipment to the top of my truck.

Most inventors would have given up after a setback such as this, but Thomas wasn't finished with the snoring problem. A few weeks later, he came walking down our driveway carrying a large parcel. My wife rushed out to greet him; obviously she had been visited by the big boat in the fog since we retired the bungee nostril pullers. She was definitely ready to fit another death trap to my face, if it meant getting some sleep.

Thomas had certainly outdone himself with the new anti-snoring gadget. He had taken a large water cannon, the kind used by kids, and had somehow refitted it into what he called "The Cringe Nose Bazooka." The cannon was pretty well stock, the only modification being two small nozzles adapted to the barrel. I could take a wild guess as to where the little nozzles went. The nose bazooka was filled with a special anti-snoring agent that Thomas would not, or could not identify. Not only would this stuff stop my snoring for an entire night, but by lucky chance, Thomas had found out that it would also extinguish a grease fire. I was starting to have my doubts, but my wife seemed all too eager to give it a try.

Thomas had written the instructions on a napkin from the local sports bar and that night, I stood before the mirror and began the procedure. I inserted the nozzles into the appropriate nostrils and I pumped the barrel of the bazooka once. I obviously wasn't ready for the sheer force; one nozzle blew free and the contents strafed the shower curtain. The other load hit the back of my throat and stuck there in a big glob. It was a little uncomfortable but I did feel like it opened up my airways somewhat. I felt lucky that half the charge was hanging on the shower curtain, although my wife thought that I should go ahead and take another shot like a man. I did not feel that I was ready for the full dosage.

Well, the Cringe Nose Bazooka did work to a certain extent. The problem was that it wore off too quickly. I'm not absolutely positive, but I believe that my wife was medicating me during the night. Some mornings, I would wake up with my head stuck to the pillow and my eyes glued shut. I would vaguely remember having a dream sometime during the night, and in this dream a wild woman was straddling me in bed. She was energetically pumping a large water cannon, taking dead aim at my face, and displaying all the inaccuracies of a half-crazed, sleep-deprived woman. When questioned about this, my wife replied that it was just a nightmare and reminded me to get in touch with Mr. Cringe. We were out of anti-snoring agent.

Unfortunately, Thomas forgot the formula for the agent which may be just as well; I was developing a rash over sixty percent of my body. The bazooka now resides on our kitchen wall where any residue left in it will combat the next grease fire.

Nocturnal habits also include unwanted movement. Once again, the married male displays a state of denial when confronted with these accusations, and we question our wives on the validity of their claims. She could have gotten those bruises down at the local supermarket during double coupon days, or at that special sale they had on women's clothing at the mall. (This event resembles a cattle drive after a close lightning strike.) There is absolutely no way that we, the average married male, can move around that much when we are asleep.

My wife was determined to prove her point. One night, I walked into our bedroom to find my wife setting up some video recording equipment. I was completely overjoyed and I anticipated a turning point in the intimate part of our marriage. Never have I loved, or felt closer to my wife than at that moment. You talk about excited. I became Christmas-morning excited and once again, we had to put the paper bag over my head for the hyperventilation. I told her that I didn't care, this meant too much to our marriage; go ahead and film us, bag and all. I also indicated that if we go easy, maybe the eye holes in the paper bag will stay in the right place. She responded that I should smarten up; the camera was there to record my sleeping habits only. I told her it didn't matter what she called it and if was okay with her, I would like to be the director.

It is sad to say, but the recording equipment was there for the documentation of my nocturnal behaviour, and I must confess that the results were quite revealing. Over the course of a few nights, a whole different Dr. Murray Dick came to light. Yes, there were the 283 different sounds that came out of my mouth; each one distinct and dissimilar to the last one. Some were incredibly serene and tranquil, others so morbid and gruesome that it was a wonder I didn't wake myself up in fright. All in all, it was like watching a National Geographic Special on TV, one where they span the entire globe filming different species of wildlife. And yes, every once in a while the big boat in the fog would put into port, and everything from my wife's sternum to the video camera would vibrate uncontrollably.

And indeed, there was movement; unwanted, nocturnal movement. There was the usual tossing and turning, and also getting out of bed and flossing the chicken wing fragments out of my teeth while I was still asleep. The camera also recorded me singing Mel Torme songs into the mirror. (I always thought that I sounded like Mel, but I didn't think that I was a fanatic.)

The main objective of my wife's filming became apparent in one of the recordings. I have always wanted to be a professional hockey goaltender, and I would have been, if not for the fact that a hockey puck frightens me. Also, any type of physical exertion tends to tire me out quite quickly. It seems that I could play an entire game while asleep, and if I had any doubts about reaching the professional level, they were put to rest with my display in the recording. I had all the moves and I could cover the whole bed.

I must point out that not only did I play goalie in bed, but I provided play by play for the entire game. You talk about excitement—I could bring the crowd to a fever pitch with my commentary, often referring to myself as the worlds' greatest goalie, and never allowing a goal during the entire game. I would have thought that my constant talking would be upsetting to my wife, but she was actually very happy. As she put it, "At least I knew when a kick save was coming."

I don't think that I have ever been more proud of my darling wife than when I was viewing the hockey games in bed. We are well aware of Gretzky being agile enough to slip checks, but I have never seen anyone as elusive as my wife in the sack. She has cat-like reflexes, and is nimble enough to throw the odd elbow every once in a while.

Before we close the book on nocturnal habits, let me say that there are some wonderful products on the market these days to combat snoring, and unlike the inventions of old Thomas Cringe, there is not a lot of fear involved in using them. My brother-in-law Wally is presently working on a thesis for the cause and cure of unwanted movement. Wally, an out-of-work master plumber who, as you know, likes to dabble in psychiatry, is unable to conduct any Primer Field

Studies for a year because of a court order. Fortunately, this hasn't stopped him from attacking the problem with his fertile mind.

After much deep thought, Wally concludes that night time wandering and movement could be the result of either a deep emotional psychotic disturbance in the psyche, or too much beer, pizza, and chicken wings before bedtime. We both realize that this could devastate an entire family, so we are hoping that the cause is the emotional thing.

Because *The Primer* is an ongoing work, I will continue to research this, as well as every other marriage problem that arises. As previously stated, I encounter new problems every day. At this point in time, we have no successful solution to the Nocturnal Habits of the Married Male but you have my word on this; I will not sleep a wink until I come up with the answer—and neither will my wife.

The Young Male's Marriage Primer
Lesson Seven
Raising Children

Dr. Murray Dick

The more astute apprentice, after glancing at The Primer Curriculum, will immediately notice that I have placed the lessons on raising children and your pet dog back-to-back. This is done for good reason as there are quite a few similarities in both techniques. When I was developing the revolutionary tools required in dealing with these subjects, one basic hypothesis was born, a theory most worthy of consideration as the student works his way through both lessons. The Primer Philosophy (TPP) on raising your pet and kids is as stated:

You can gain the love and trust from your children and your dog, using money and puppy dog treats, in that order.

Let us begin our lesson on raising children. There is a great possibility that the Young Male perusing this chapter has no kids, and quite possibly, may never have any. This is no excuse for skipping on to raising dogs. At some time in your married life, every male is exposed to young children; in visiting them, coaching them, babysitting them, or just chasing them off your front lawn. It is a wise man who begins his training early in dealing with children.

And it is training. Men are not naturally equipped for this kind of interaction; they cannot deal with the unknown, and most aspects of young children remain unknown because they either cannot, or they will not, communicate. We are used to the guy at the sports bar giving us a subtle, but ample warning that he is about to be sick, granting us time to move our chicken wings to safety. A baby cannot do this and our first indication of a child's stomach ailment is, quite often, a load of pabulum in the shirt pocket.

I realize that young children are going to get sick, but it would be nice if they had a warning system of some kind to enable you to get the child into the bathroom and over the toilet. Down at the local sports bar, we have a foolproof system to warn us of any upcoming stomach disorders.

Picture us sitting there, with the only sound being the relentless munching of chicken wings, and the occasional slurp of a cold beer. Suddenly, there is a low rumble. It is a noise comparable to that of a garbage compactor in your sink, one that you have dangerously overfilled. In a flash, the patrons are on alert and in surveillance mode. Everyone glances at his table buddy (the one next to him), for the dreaded signs of nausea—staring straight down at his food, and profusely sweating more than usual. When someone is found who meets this criterion, his table buddy yells out, "Got 'im."

He then places his ear close to the patient's mouth to discern how much time we have, and also to judge the severity of the event. By calculating the volume and the frequency of the rumbles, he either announces, "It's a mild one, we've got plenty of time to clear away from the table," or in a severe case, he may have only enough time to yell, "We've got three seconds before he blows! Save yourselves."

Be aware that the initial eruption may not be the end of the episode. After everything has been wiped down and someone has gone outside to find the waitresses, you still have to be wary of aftershocks. These are usually silent and can be just as hazardous. The guys call them second helpings.

Women do remarkably well in the training of children, and until recently, no one understood why. It was Wally who unlocked the secret behind this mystery. I know of no man who manages his time like my brother-in-law. Even with all the travel involved in his out-of-work master plumber business, he still finds time to dabble in psychiatry. He informed me that he came across an article in a DNA magazine at the local barbershop. It spoke of research confirming the presence of a special parenting gene, a gene found only in women. It is located right next to the shopping gene which, if you recall, allows a woman to shop the malls for days without rest or sustenance. This is stunning research data to say the least. Wally is truly one of today's real thinkers.

Flushed with the success of the gene theory, Wally has authored yet another pamphlet, branching into the world of child psychiatry. It is simply called, *A Child's Mind, I Know it Well*. To keep with the infant theme, he has written it in different colours of crayons. In one remarkable section, Wally tells the heartbreaking, but equally uplifting classic story, "The Little Toilet Plunger That Could." The accompanying illustrations will move you beyond belief. To see that little plunger going up and down in the toilet, all the while saying "I think I can, I think I can," will bring tears to your eyes. I don't want to spoil the ending for you but the little plunger indeed "could."

I first thought of the problems of raising children well before we had our own. I felt that a prepared father had an edge on someone who starts the learning of this all-important task after the fact. I had some brilliant ideas but no one to experiment on. Luckily, my sister had a young child and because she allowed us to baby-sit him, I began to hone my techniques on my small nephew of two years of age.

My first observation was that he could not express himself very well. The goo-goos and da-das did not make a whole lot of sense to me, and I was afraid that this kind of communication might hold him back later in his chosen career. The solution was both brilliant and functional.

I taught him to bark like a puppy dog. In the three weeks that we watched him, he developed a highly sophisticated mode of communication, yelping crisply when I held a baby cookie out to him, and even barking numerous times when he wanted more than one. His motor skills showed a remarkable improvement. How many toddlers can shake a paw at that early an age, or even roll over on command? When he begged for food by holding up his tiny hands in front of him, it was just the cutest little thing you ever saw.

They say that a baby becomes imprinted by certain experiences in his life, and I am proud to say that the dog routine stayed with my nephew for years. I believe that he was nine or ten years old when he ran away from home for the fiftieth time and demanded to talk to a dog-catcher.

This wasn't my last wonderful teaching experience with my nephew. A few years later, my sister called and said that her son could not go to his Cub Scouts father-and-son banquet because her husband had to work late. She was desperate, having approached everyone that she knew. She even asked a few strangers on the street if they would substitute for his father. All else had failed; I was her last hope. I was thrilled that my sister had chosen me ahead of all others, and of course, I would take my little six-year-old nephew to the dinner.

It was on the ride to the banquet that I had my first emotional talk with a child. He asked me why his daddy would not take him. How do you tell a little boy that his daddy wanted to take him more than the whole wide world? How do you tell him that sometimes grown-ups have to work long hours to support their family? When he is looking up at you with tears in his little eyes, you can't tell him these things. You just can't. So I told him his dad had to go to prison for awhile, but could take visitors on weekends.

To lighten the mood, I asked my nephew if he wanted to do something special as a surprise for his mother. He immediately cheered up when I enquired if he had ever thought about getting a tattoo. I explained what a tattoo was and he became all excited, saying that he loved cars and would like a "hot rod" on his chest. I dropped him off at the local parlor with some money while I took the opportunity to do some power tool shopping.

When I picked him up and he showed me his tattoo, I immediately sensed a communication problem between my nephew and the tattooist. It must have been the pronunciation. Instead of a hot rod, he now had a 'hot broad' inked into his little chest. He pointed and asked, "Are these the headlights?"

I replied, "Well, sort of."

The time and effort that I put into helping raise my nephew was not lost on my sister. She has been moved to the point of speechlessness for many years, and to this very day, she still cannot find the words to thank me. When someone mentions the little scar-marks on my nephew's chest, where the tattoo was surgically removed, my sister leaves the room immediately. I think she leaves to cry.

I was now confident in my capabilities as a father, and when our own children arrived, I lent a very strong hand in their upbringing. I have been blessed with two gorgeous daughters, each with their own personalities, but both with my wife's good looks. (A point gained in the point system.) Let me give the Young Male an overall view of fathers who have daughters. It has been said that we are over-protective, and in a sense this is true. Over-protective is just a brief stopover for us on our way to becoming murderous.

A man with sons will come into work and announce, "Gee, that little Billy of mine, he went out on a date last night, and he did this, and he did that. Boy, what a 'chip off the old block', he-he."

Fathers of daughters are not likely to come into work and say this. We are more apt to say, "Gee, I heard that little Billie tried something last night with my daughter and she gave him a well-placed knee. I think she took a chip off the old block, he-he."

My oldest daughter was my first attempt at raising my own child. I single handedly raised that girl with a lot of help from my wife. She was my little princess and I protected her, always there in times of need—unless, of course, I was busy in my workshop or down at the local sports bar. The early years were wonderful.

One day it all changed. I was outside watching my wife cut the grass when I decided we could both use a cold drink of iced tea. I glanced in the back window and recoiled in terror. I raced out to my wife and I shouted over the roar of her lawn mower, "There's a strange man sitting across from our daughter at the kitchen table."

My wife replied. "He's not a stranger. He's little Billie from down the road and he's not a man. He's six years of age—just like our daughter. Go sit in the garden and relax."

Well, I did go and sit in the garden, but I did not relax. My parenting world, as I knew it, was coming to an end. As I sat there amongst the cucumbers and zucchini-squash, I realized that deep down within my soul, I always knew that this day would come—the day when my little princess was no longer just Daddy's little girl. I stood at a crossroads. I could fight this maturing process with all my might or I could accept it, sharing her life and the many new experiences to come.

I slowly rose and knocked the potato beetles off my trousers. I would share the future with my daughter, and I would start by accepting this fine young man into our home. I entered the kitchen, walked over to the little boy and asked, "Who are you, and just what do you think you're doing here?"

"Daddy, he's little Billie from down the road," my daughter replied.

"Well, maybe little Billie from down the road, if that's his real name, can answer his own questions," I responded with sensitivity.

"I am little Billie from down the road and I'm helping your daughter with her homework," he slyly replied.

I sensed a filthy lie. "My daughter gets straight A's, so let's not use that one. Maybe you're here because you have a galloping hormone. That's right, I used to have one of those and I know exactly what you're thinking about this very minute. Do you have any stocks and bonds? How do you plan on supporting my daughter? Maybe you had better go home and expand your paper route."

My daughter ran out the back door. "Mommy, Daddy's scaring us again."

Years later, when I look back and see how well my daughter turned out, I know that I made the right decision that day. Gaining her trust with open dialogue was not unlike the communications that I have with my wife. I cannot stress this enough to the Young Males who are considering starting a family. You must allow your children to grow, but be there beside them.

I was there beside my oldest daughter during her dating years. When an outstanding young gentleman rang the door bell, it was me that welcomed him into our house. It was always me who made him feel comfortable and at home by offering him a soda pop, some potato chips, perhaps a cold shower, or even a casual death-threat should he try anything. How many fathers care this much about their daughters and the friends they spend time with?

My eldest never thanked me. Like her mother, she could find no words to express her appreciation. She would sometimes become so emotional that she would rush from the room before the tears of gratitude would overcome her. If the student takes but one bit of advice from this lesson, let it be this: You, as a parent, can take part in your children's activities without being stifling or smothering. I am living proof of that.

I was my oldest daughter's date for her senior prom. She went on and on about how it was not necessary, and how she already had an escort, but I insisted. Making the phone call to disappoint the young man was perhaps the hardest thing I have ever done. How do you tell the star quarterback on the senior team that he was being replaced? How do you tell a young man, who had just recently obtained a full football scholarship to a Big Ten school, that his girlfriend would rather accompany her father to the dance? Well, you can't. You just can't.

So I told him that she had diarrhea, not the occasional kind, but the severe stuff. This seemed to placate him, and just as a side note, he recently signed a multi-million dollar contract with a pro football team. If he is reading this, and I'm sure he is, let me just say thanks for helping a young lady achieve her dream on prom night.

I borrowed a suit from my brother-in-law Wally, and although he is eight inches shorter than me, I don't think that the white socks stood out all that much. We did not rent a limo, but in order to transport all my daughter's friends, I borrowed a station wagon from a patron of the local sports bar who sometimes used it to transport chickens. Luckily for us, he was taking the weekend off. It turned out that the extra car space was not needed; all of my daughter's little friends already had rides. Actually, a lot of them cancelled their entire prom for some reason.

It's a shame that my oldest daughter came down with a sickness shortly after entering the dance. We had to leave a little bit early—about thirty seconds after arrival. I was disappointed because I think that we stood a good chance of being named Prom Queen and Prom Dad. She said that it was probably the flu, but it might have been a chicken feather allergy. I thought that I had vacuumed everything out of the station wagon, but after I turned the defroster on, it became quite fluffy inside the car.

It is important to note here that children are greatly influenced by the accomplishments of their parents. After years of hard work and dedication, our oldest daughter went into medicine. I think it is fair to say that she got her passion for education from her father. If I remember correctly, I graduated on the dean's list in my grade-eight year. (I don't think it hurt that I lent the teacher my mustache wax.)

Finally, there was the day when she brought home a young man for us to meet. After the greeting formalities and the offers of a soda pop, chips, strip search, and so on, the conversation got around to his vocation. He was an electrical engineer.

There is a staggering statistic that states: "Every thirty minutes, a Canadian is jolted in an electrical accident." That Canadian is me. I don't know why—maybe it's because I can never find my tester, or maybe it's the confusion about the black and white wires. The truth is I have been trying to re-wire my basement for twenty-five years. I have been hampered by frequent trips to the emergency room where I have my own bed.

After hearing of this young man's profession, I retired to the kitchen and returned with some soda pop, chips, and a marriage certificate that I had been saving for such a joyous occasion. Today, our little doctor and her electrical engineer husband live a happy coexistence near Toronto. He is an outstanding young gentleman, and I have had numerous high quality visits with him in my basement.

I believe that the Young Male now has an idea of the effort that goes into quality parenting. It is imperative that you become part of your child's life. You should not expect to have the same success as I have achieved in child-raising. However, someday you may be sitting in your own garden, and there, amongst the green beans and chili peppers, the decision will have to be made. Make the right one for your children's sake.

The raising of my youngest daughter was somewhat different. The following lesson may seem like a long, winding narrative, but by bearing with me, the Young Male will eventually see how power tools can help in the upbringing of an adolescent.

I guess every family has a rebel, a child who searches for his or her own identity. I remember looking in old photo albums to see if any of my ancestors had a nose ring, and I believe my youngest was the first, and so far, the only one. I could be wrong, a couple of pictures looked promising, but it may have been the fading of the photographs with age, or a growth of some kind.

When our oldest daughter left for university, our youngest came into her own. Her job around the house was to make sure it did not become too quiet and calm. She was very good at her work. I became all too familiar with phrases such as "the calm before the storm," the ever-popular "pushing one's buttons," and the "rattling of the chain."

For instance, my wife and I might be sitting in the living room reading the paper, and my daughter would come in. She would sit down, and for a few short minutes she would assess the situation. This was the calm. In short order, she would start pushing the buttons.

"I've been thinking about getting a Harley Davidson tattoo on my butt."

Once again we would return to the calm. The only sound for a few minutes was the rustle of the newspaper as my wife clenched and unclenched her hands.

All too soon the calm was shattered by her mother, who appeared rattled. "Well, we're not letting you get a motorcycle tattoo on your butt, and that's final."

"Well, it's my butt," my daughter pushed.

"I diapered your butt for many-a-good year and you're not getting a tattoo on it."

And away they'd go. I felt it prudent to go out to my workshop and come back later when the dust had settled. I returned in one hour and there they were, sitting beside each other, laughing at a TV show. I never did figure this out.

I believe the rebel streak was at its strongest when our youngest began dating. As in the case of her sister, I would meet these boys at the door and try not to stare at the body piercings or the tattoos. It is a sad commentary when you judge a young man by how many times you want to beat him up. "Well that was a nice young gentleman; much better than the last one. I only wanted to thump this guy twice."

Looking back, I realized that they were also rebels, also searching for their own identity, and also fine young men. I just didn't want them searching at our front door at that particular time.

As I was coming home one day, I spotted a strange car in our driveway. I hoped that it wasn't a new boyfriend, but at least the vehicle was not an old VW van with "Death to the Establishment" painted on the side. I opened the door of the house and the first thing I noticed was a pair of shoes. I have large feet—size thirteen. These were at least three sizes bigger and they easily dwarfed my own.

I was standing there, staring in utter amazement when a terrible, horrifying thought occurred to me. Oh no, our daughter's gone and done it now—she's dating the giant from the circus! I wasn't up to this kind of confrontation so I started to quietly back out the door. But it was too late.

"Dad, could you come into the living room?" It was her sing-song voice, the one she used whenever she was extremely happy and wanted my approval. I feared the worst. I feared that she was about to tell me of her plan to run away and join the circus, to be close to her new boyfriend. As I slowly made my way into the house, my thoughts raced. Would the giant approve of me and only thump me twice? Has he put his feet up and through my coffee table? Were there any groceries left in the house? How's our chandelier doing?

I rounded the corner of the living room and was met by the shining, grinning face of my daughter. Again, she used her special sing-song voice.

"Dad, I'd like you to meet Billy."

A young man arose from the couch, and he actually finished standing up a few inches shorter than me. He was clean-shaven, his hair was of modest length and well groomed. He had no visible tattoos, and if he had any piercings, they were out of sight. He was a fine looking young man.

Before we could shake hands or say anything, my daughter blurted out, "Billy owns a whole bunch of power tools."

Well, of all the sneaky, low-down tricks. How shallow and gullible did she think I was? But when it comes to power tools, I do not take chances, so I immediately hugged the lad. Later, Billy and I were laughing and giggling on the couch as we leafed through the latest Tools 'R Us catalogue. It suddenly occurred to me that I still did not know his last name. I usually run a police check on all my daughters' boyfriends.

When he told me his last name, I immediately recognized it from Gus's Lumber and Marriage Manual Store. His father was a regular visitor. You will not find better folks than those who frequent lumber stores, and once again, we were hugging and dancing in the middle of the room.

This seemed all too good to be true. My wife and I welcomed this young man with open arms, but there was one brief moment when we thought that this good thing was coming to an end.

Billy lived in Calgary, Alberta, quite a distance from our small Southern Ontario town. My daughter had flown out to visit him and we were waiting for her return at the airport. As she walked inside, we could see the tears rolling down her face, and we could hear her sobbing and crying.

My wife was visibly upset, "Oh no, they've broken up."

I immediately replied, "Now hold on there dear. Let's not jump to conclusions. Maybe she just cracked her head on the luggage rack, or maybe she got into some bad airline food. But don't worry, if they have broken up, I'll start the adoption proceedings for the boy tomorrow."

Well, it turned out that it was none of the above; they had not broken up, and she hadn't bumped her head. She was just missing her man, and it seems that our rebel—our tough little button pusher, had missed her man so much that she had been crying all the way from Calgary, a four-hour flight. And by the way, wouldn't that be a treat for the person sitting beside her?

Today, she doesn't miss him anymore. They are happily married, and I have two wonderful grandchildren who I plan on helping to raise into fine little human beings, using my revolutionary Primer techniques, of course.

In closing, let me summarize a few key points in this lesson. It is imperative that the Young Male begin his child raising training immediately. You need to do it right now, while it is fresh in your mind—not in a few minutes, when you have forgotten. I did not wait until we had our own kids. I found that practicing on a close relative's child helped me immensely in honing my technique. A close relative is better than a friend, because a relative may be less likely to take you to court.

Be protective, but not smothering. Take an interest in your children and include yourself in every facet of their life, whether they like it or not.

Finally, look for the good in all of your children's friends. You cannot judge people by face value alone, as I found out with my youngest daughter. When I think of all of those strange looking young men that rang our doorbell, and the way I treated each one with dignity and respect, I can feel very, very proud of myself.

If the student recalls, I started the last segment of this lesson by stating that power tools can help in the upbringing of a child. As you can see, it can also help with the most important choice a person will ever make; choosing a spouse, as my youngest has shown. There is a wise old adage that I just recently made up. "You have to look deep inside to find the good in people—deep inside their garage."

The Young Male's Marriage Primer
Lesson Eight
Raising Your Pet Dog

Dr. Murray Dick

Is there anything more precious than a cuddly little puppy dog bringing your slippers to you, or what's left of them?
A leading dog scientist, tops in his field

Once again, I begin a lesson with a quote from a leading scientist who, as anyone can easily see, is tops in his field. Sooner or later, most Young Males will get a dog for family fun and enjoyment. In this lecture, we will cover the proper selection and maintenance of your new pet. You may ask, "Why a dog and not a cat?" Well, cats are impossible to train, extremely hard on the furniture, and tend to stray from home. Your wife already has someone like this.

You must use good judgment in choosing your new pet because it can, and will, affect your marriage. Be selective in your choice of a dog because the companionship of a puppy can last a lifetime, with little or no chance of parole. Once again, I will be using one of my patented teaching techniques, that being Teaching by Example—showcasing the cutting-edge "dog-raising" technology that I have developed for *The Primer*. The versatility built into my marriage manual is one of its strengths. My revolutionary concepts are designed first and foremost for human beings, but are easily adapted to cover pets, farm animals, and even woodland creatures if so desired.

As in past chapters, I will be calling on my brother-in-law for some sound advice. Wally, an out-of-work master plumber who, as you know, likes to dabble in psychiatry, will give us his latest insights regarding the world of animal behaviour. Never one to rest on his laurels, Wally has branched off into canine psychology. Some time ago, he gathered a pack of dogs for study—mostly strays and drop-offs. He was forced to abandon his mission prematurely because of a new bylaw recently passed in town—one regarding offensive odours emanating from Wally's home, where he was housing a pack of dogs. Nevertheless, look for wise words from this multi-talented man at the conclusion of the lesson.

Let me begin by saying that in my forty or so years of marriage, I have owned many dogs, and I have categorized them as follows. We have had dogs that were smart and gentle, and also those that were stupid and vicious. There were some that were smart and vicious, and the odd one that was stupid and gentle. I have owned dogs that showed great gentleness for the sole purpose of lulling me into a sense of security, only to turn vicious when I let my guard down. Some canines started out smart and then turned stupid for no apparent reason, while others started stupid from day one and carried this inherent trait for their entire lives.

Before you jump to any conclusions, such as never wanting to own a vicious dog, let me just say that there can be a bright side to this. We once had a stupid, vicious dog that nipped my wife's hand every time she tried to scratch his belly. Actually, this worked out rather well for me. If there is any belly scratching going on in our house, I like to be in on it and I'm not stupid. I don't bite, and I lie real still.

We once had a smart, vicious cur that got upset because I blamed him for something he did not do. When my wife asked me who tracked sawdust in from the workshop, I pointed to the dog. Dogs cannot talk so I figured that I had beaten the rap, but I failed to take into consideration his intelligence. The dog briefly left the room and returned, carrying one of my work boots in his teeth. It was covered in sawdust. I swear that I could almost hear that tattle-tale of a dog laughing at me. He then showed his viciousness by sneaking into my bedroom that night and biting me on the neck. I am a sound sleeper because of heavy snacking just before bedtime, and I cannot prove beyond a reasonable doubt that it was the dog that bit me. However, I do know a little about forensic science, and I concluded that the teeth marks did not match up with anyone else in the family, plus no one else had motive that week. Man's best friend—yeah, right!

This went on for about a week; the dog continued to gnaw away at me every night. Not enough to break the skin—he was too smart for that—just enough to cause an irritation. My wife said that it looked like spider bites, probably caused by sleep walking. I asked her how this would cause me to have a run-in with a spider, and she replied that during the night I often end up on the back lawn because I can't find the fridge in my sleep.

My brother-in-law Wally rigged up a battery-operated shocking device that was attached to the vicious dog's collar. At the appropriate time (when I sensed an attack), I would press a remote button that would activate a mild and harmless shock. The very first night we tried the experiment, my wife reported hearing a great deal of activity near the dog's bed. It seems that I was rolling on the remote every once in a while. Interestingly enough, the vicious cur was very well behaved the next few days, partly because of the desired effect of the training device, and also because he had to sleep all day. My wife finally made me take the collar off the dog when she caught me using it to entertain guests one evening.

I would like to take a little time to tell you about our present dog, a supposedly purebred yellow Labrador retriever, and a tough dog to categorize. She is very gentle, and when it comes to food, she is very intelligent. In other aspects of life, she displays no desire to learn. My family claims that she is still a puppy, but we must face the facts; she's over six years old and she has grown large enough for a small man to ride. I believe that there is something far more complicated at work in this dog's brain.

For instance, she cannot or will not sit, heel, or roll over. However, I have watched as she constructed an access ramp to the very top of the bird feeder using only firewood and lumber scavenged from my workshop—an impressive display of engineering by all accounts. Yet this is the same dog that has never grasped the concept of shade. She lies in direct sunlight on a hot summer's day, panting and sweating profusely through her tongue. I like to think that we were making some headway last summer, but the onslaught of autumn put a halt to any progress. Nevertheless, I have always been one to work with my canine, and next year we will carry on, perhaps bringing in a neighbour's cow as a training aid for the proper use of shade.

The dog will not come if you call her name, "Bailey." You must use her entire name, "Bailey, would you like a treat?" This brings us to the puppy dog bones. Bailey refuses to stay at home. Someone got the idea that if I were to carry treats in my pocket, the dog would stick around the house. This is all well and good when we are walking around the property, as she stays glued to your side, poking at your pockets for the little treasures inside. But as you know, I run a lucrative at-home woodworking business, and there is nothing worse than a big dog ramming into you continuously when you are operating a large, powerful table saw. While this alone seriously compromises my safety ethic in the shop, it does get worse.

Her lack of common sense prohibits her from learning where pockets start and where they end. To her, a person has as many pockets on the front of their pants as on the sides. I have had to post a sign at the front door for purely legal reasons: "Beware of dog. She is going to head-butt you a good one, so do not meet her face on. Please greet the dog sideways." I really cannot stress this enough. The dog's head weighs about twenty-five pounds and she has another seventy pushing from behind, so she will get your attention. Nothing says welcome like your dog doubling a guest over in pain.

Another undesirable trait that this dog possesses is her ability to find dead things scattered around the countryside. She seems to have acquired all the homing instincts of a vulture, without the scavenger's ability to digest something that is well past its expiry date. Vultures would have gone extinct eons ago had they been susceptible to the kinds of stomach disorders that this dog gets. Usually, they occur in the middle of the night, and the dog, not wanting to bother anyone, wanders down to the sunroom and notices all the stars through the wrap-around windows. Her train of thought is as follows: "Hey, I must be in the backyard. I think I'll do it right here." In the morning it is easy to think that this is the home where the buffalo roam.

However, the biggest disappointment in this dog is her swimming ability, or lack thereof. I watched as she timidly walked around our backyard pool, and I wondered why she wasn't jumping in. After all, a yellow lab is a retriever, bred for hunting, and swimming should be second nature to this dog. This behaviour went on for a few weeks until I finally threw her in. I found out that the dog does not swim very well. Her front half has this wild doggie paddle going on—her paws crash up and down on the surface. Her back half has absolutely nothing going on—her rear end slowly sinks down until she is almost vertical in the water. This causes her front paws to just wave in the air. All the while, she has this look in her eyes that seems to say, "Ah, I need a little help here, I'm floundering." The only positive thing to come out of this entire swimming fiasco is that our family has been forced to keep our Red Cross lifesaving up to date. Sometimes late at night, I think of what might have happened if a hunter had bought this dog. I sleep well knowing that I saved a little puppy dog's life.

Our dog Bailey will retrieve on dry land however. She is very adept at bringing back a Frisbee, although it's pretty well chewed up by the time she returns, and it doesn't fly right thereafter. Let's say that she did belong to a duck hunter and maybe she did learn to swim. I firmly believe she would retrieve a newly-shot duck and would not eat it in transit. It wouldn't be dead enough for that dog.

The majority of the Young Males probably won't remember, but there was an old TV show that my generation watched. Each week on "Lassie," little Timmy would get into some kind of life-threatening situation and his faithful, intelligent collie would save his life every single time. More importantly, Lassie never got muddy from the neighbour's field, she most certainly did not eat like a vulture, and she would not yelp for help if she accidentally fell into the farm pond.

The show was a smash hit for years, but as I gained maturity from raising my own children, I found myself questioning the reality of the program. I believe that it showcased shoddy parenting. Little Timmy would run by his mother on the way outside and say, "I'm going out to play by the well with no top on it."

His mother would reply, "That's nice Timmy. Make sure you wear your jacket."

Week after week, he would fall into that well. Every Thursday night in prime time, Lassie would either run for help or haul him out in the bucket. There was another character on the show called Gramps because he was older and, more than likely, because he was the grandpa. We tend to equate older people with sensibility and wisdom gained through years of experience; but Gramps would say, "I see Timmy's playing by the well with no top on it; I hope he's got his jacket on because it's probably pretty chilly down at the bottom." I think you can see what I mean—there was no parental guidance going on at all.

Timmy obviously had issues and he was not your typical teeter-totter kind of kid. Daredevil children need a strong authority presence, and unfortunately he wasn't getting this. I sometimes wonder how little Timmy made out later in life. I certainly hope there was no open-top wells at his place of employment; accidents in the workplace not only reduce production, but can raise costly insurance premiums.

And let's talk about Lassie. If this dog was so smart, why did she put up with this stuff every week? If she was that smart, why didn't she come into the house, knock the telephone off the cradle and use her little paw to call the Children's Aid Society? It would have been an open-and-shut case. I am quite sure, that by using the latest scientific technology, a sharp prosecutor could match the bruises and contusions on little Timmy's body to the contours of the well walls. Sometimes it amazes me that I am the only one to ever pick up on these things.

Lassie was no young pup either; she was getting up there in dog years. She probably wanted nothing more than to lie on the porch, do some inappropriate licking, and drool all over herself. This brings up another issue, Lassie never drooled. Every dog that we have ever owned drooled—not just the perspiration dripping off of its tongue, I mean the long stringy stuff that just grows out of the corner of their mouths until it almost reaches the carpet. It just hangs there, bouncing and swinging like a bungee chord. No one in our family ever had the stomach to relieve the dog of this "hanger," and it was left to old Dad to fix up the dog's face. I would get my hockey stick out and knock the drool off. I don't remember little Timmy ever getting his hockey stick out.

But life goes on as does this lesson. I have always wondered if our dog Bailey would run for help, should I ever fall in a well. We do have an old well in the backyard and I thought about experimenting, but I'm not supposed to go near it. It has a heavy cement lid that my wife can barely lift. Treating it as a hypothetical question, and after careful consideration, I have come to the conclusion that Bailey would go for help under certain circumstances. I would have to get the puppy dog bone out of my pocket and throw it in the general vicinity of help. This would have to be done quickly as I was falling, but before actually entering the well.

I realize that this would be extremely difficult, even for a gifted athlete such as me. Should I go down with the puppy dog bone still in my pocket, a different state of affairs would take place. I would be closely followed by a hundred-pound dog, nipping at my pants, and adding more complexity to an already serious situation. If perchance, I survive the fall and the dog landing on my head, I would still have to tread water with one hand while holding the dog afloat with the other, all the while staying clear of her air-beating front paws. This is not a scenario I choose to think of very often, but it would have made a great story line on "Lassie."

Before the Young Males think that I've given up on Bad Dog Bailey because of all the awful things I have just related, let me remind you that I do like to work with my canine. As my brother-in-law Wally so wisely states, "There's a silver lining behind every crowd." I have consulted him on the abnormal behaviour of this dog and he has lent his skilled, cutting-edge dog expertise to this problem.

Wally, ever the optimist, sees potential for our current yellow lab. He feels that if puppy dog bones ever become an illegal substance, and who is to say they won't, Bailey will always have a job at the airport. She will be most adept at seeking out and finding any contraband puppy dog bones, and punishing the dastardly offenders right on the spot—especially if they are smuggling stuff in their front pocket.

Personally, I would be happy if the dog were to obtain employment at a ski resort during avalanche week. Merely handing out puppy dog bones at the entrance of the lift would ensure swift and speedy recovery, should someone become buried in a snow slide. Resort staff would then haul the dog off to ensure that the lucky survivor is not poked to death.

Finally Young Males, the owning and maintenance of a pet is not much different than the raising of small children, a topic covered earlier in *The Primer*. Think of raising your pet as training for the future when those little kiddies are taking over your heart.

A dog will be good and perform for a reward. This does not make him any different than the married male, and I highlight this theme when I address the Young Married Females in my seminars: *"Ladies, don't forget the love, don't forget the food, and don't forget the belly scratches. Your man deserves as much and will respond accordingly."*

My thanks go out to my-brother-in law Wally, a man who I confide in so much—a man who did not hesitate to take time off from his successful career as an out-of-work master plumber to help make this lesson the success I know it is. Although he had the stray dogs and drop-offs for only a short time in his house, the data he was able to gather was priceless and his deductions were stunning. This experience will enable him to jump off into animal husbandry, or something like that in the future. Bear in mind that it is not only the raw data that is important here; Wally will have emotional memories and stuff like that for years to come. When you enter Wally's home, you can sense that something wonderful happened here; something that the average married male can never appreciate unless you have lived it, and something that stays with you for days, even weeks. It is something that neither time nor numerous steam cleanings can ever put asunder.

Let me wish the Young Male success in the raising of his pet dog.

The Young Male's Marriage Primer
Lesson Nine
The Dreamboat Husband Award

Dr. Murray Dick

Recently I painted the kitchen. I thought that I would go with a paisley tint and avocado overtones, topped off with just a hint of glazing to highlight the contours of the walls. These colours were chosen because together, they are both harmonious and calming. Upon completion, I accessorized the space with ultra-modern fixtures bordering on French provincial. For window treatments, I chose sheer drapes with cascading flutes that shimmered as they slightly puddle on the floor. All in all, the space turned out to be very pleasing. Alas, it was wonderful eye candy and the completed project was quite Avon-guard, if I do say so myself.

Ha! I had you going there for a moment, didn't I? You have just read some Primer Humour, humourous in the fact that I, as a husband, might have some taste when it comes to home decorating. To tell you the truth, I haven't a clue of what I just wrote. Most of it was copied from one of my wife's decorating magazines. I know only two colours—Black and Decker.

As a matter of fact, I always thought that avocados where small furry animals that lived in the woods behind our house. I taught my children not to fear the elusive avocado, but to respect this little beast. The kids were both in their early twenties before they realized that no matter how often they called, no avocado was coming out of the forest to be petted. I still have an avocado live-trap in my garage.

I think that the Young Male gets the picture. I did partake in painting the kitchen recently and I will relate the entire successful episode later in the lesson. First, I would like to comment on the title of this chapter, The Dreamboat Husband Award.

The Young Male's Marriage Primer is, in its rawest form, a survival guide to marriage. Inside its pages, the Young Male will find all the tools necessary to endure the hardships, the pitfalls, and the hazards that he will encounter along the way. This is true, providing of course, that he does his homework and dedicates his entire life to the well-being of the family—as I have done throughout my forty-one years of wedded bliss. The basics included the point system, communication, that unique something, and many more invaluable lessons.

The Primer however, is so much more. Once I found that I could help a man eke out a pathetic, modest existence with his wife, I wanted to do more. I developed special lessons to help him excel; to surpass his own potential as a feeble little husband, and to venture far beyond the normal expectations of your average married male. Simply put, I wanted to mold him into what wives so desperately desire—a dreamboat husband.

In another ground-breaking Primer Field Study (PFS) carried out down at the local sports bar, I inaugurated the Dreamboat Husband Award. The DHA is actually a wooden plaque made in my very own workshop and is awarded to any married man who performs a good deed at home—a deed that surpasses the basic acts lawfully required in any marriage. This reward system is somewhat reminiscent of The Boy Scouts badge system, only there is more beer and chicken wings present at our ceremonies.

After presenting his latest accomplishment to a panel of judges (Wally and myself), the applicant then awaits the decision. If the good deed meets the stringent criteria needed to win the coveted DHA, the judges will ponder their decision during the intermission of the hockey game, and announce their verdict following the conclusion of the match. If accepted, the lucky contestant then approaches the plaque and proceeds to write his name below the previous winner with a special pencil crayon; all the while being cheered on raucously by the envious patrons of the bar.

Let the Young Male be advised that it is no easy task to win this award. As stated during the introduction of *The Primer*, I am a tower of strength in helping around the house. But even I cannot include such mundane tasks, as dusting the remotes every day and keeping my beer fridge cleaned out, as deeds good enough to qualify for the popular DHA. No, the standards set by the panel of adjudicators can best be described as stringent. Also, be advised that the judges' decision is final.

It will come as no surprise that the inaugural winner of the dreamboat was, of course, I. The second name on the plaque belongs to my brother-in-law Wally. Wally, an out-of-work master plumber who, as you know, likes to dabble in psychiatry, did not really earn his award because he does absolutely nothing around the house. However, the hectic schedule of an out-of-work master plumber can be extremely tiring, and besides, I needed a second winner to make the DHA look somewhat official.

To illustrate the strict requirements that the applicant needs to fulfill, I will once again utilize my cutting-edge Primer tool, Teaching by Example. Call it a gift, if you will, but I have never been shy when it comes to helping out at home. I will go into great detail in describing a number of good deeds that I have personally completed around the house in an effort to help the Young Male get a sense of what is involved in reaching dreamboat status in his wife's eyes. We will begin with the kitchen painting lesson.

I believe it was two years ago that I was sitting in the sports bar and I commented to the other patrons on how clear the TV picture was. The guys informed me that it was the new satellite dish TV. I was rather amazed. Being on the old aerial all my life, I found this quite enjoyable. I could actually see the hockey puck. For the past thirty years, when watching a hockey game, I became quite adept at focusing on an area where two or more players congregated, and by logical deduction, I concluded that the puck must be in there somewhere. When a group of people wearing the same shade of uniform huddled around a net, hugged, and raised their arms, a goal must have been scored. When a bunch of guys wearing different coloured jerseys gathered together, hugged, and started flailing away at each other, I knew I was watching a good old fashioned hockey free-for-all.

It just wasn't hockey that appeared fuzzy on my old TV. A tennis game consisted of two people running around on their respective sides of the net for no apparent reason. I actually watched Baywatch for the plot—and I'm not just kidding.

The guys went on to champion this new technology and to rave about all the channels available. My brother-in-law Wally even mentioned the twenty-four-hour women's beach volleyball network that he watched—if there was nothing titillating on the Discovery or Learning Channel.

Well, this got me to thinking and eventually to planning. I developed and presented a communication to my wife on the benefits of dish TV. I started with the promise that I would spend much less time at the sports bar if I was watching the big game at home. We both knew that this was a filthy lie, and after much communicating and downright whining, I was eventually allowed to have the new dish installed. Unfortunately, she did not buy into the idea that a dish only works on a big screen TV.

My life was changed immediately, and for a while it changed in a good way. I was consumed by the variety of content available and the teaching ability of this new media tool. Like my brother-in-law Wally, I found the overall content of the Discovery and Learning Channels to be somewhat lacking at certain times. Therefore, I spent considerable time at the women's beach volleyball network, for the sole purpose of learning the rules.

It was a quiet night by my TV standards when the good times came to an abrupt end. I remember it all so clearly. I was surfing the dish (which is cool jargon for looking through the entire 400 channels), when I hit on the W network. Young Males, a word of warning, the W does not stand for wrestling. Do not stop for any length of time on this channel. When you first get your dish, put one of those parental control things on this channel. My wife, who was sitting watching me watch TV, was immediately intrigued by the W or Women's Network. This led to her own channel surfing, and before long, she had a whole list of favourites. Along with the W, there was Garden and Home, the Life Network, the Decorating Channel, the Shopping Channel, and the Fashion Network. There are also a bunch of feminist channels that you best stay away from. They included the Nag Network, the Get His Big Lazy Butt off the Couch Channel, and the Out Of Court Settlement Network where she gets Custody of All the Power Tools Channel. All in all, these channels can be very intimidating to the married male.

The decorating channels turned out to be the worst of the bunch. They stimulate a woman in such a way that upon the completion of the show, she has a multitude of new ideas to incorporate around the house. This would not be all that bad if she did these things alone. Unfortunately for us, the married male will be a part of this—meaning that after the show, you had to get up and help do stuff. You never did this after watching TV sports; mainly because you were physically unable to do anything. If you snacked properly during the game, you were pretty well paralyzed by the end, and crawling into bed was a major accomplishment. Now, we watch the decorating show and as soon as the credits roll, you are on the move. You will be asked to move the couch here, then there, and then back again. You will be pressured into putting the door back on the guest bathroom—even though it has only been off for a couple of years. You are going to go shopping for curtains which is, as every married male knows, the capital punishment of shopping. And yes, you are going to paint the kitchen.

To be honest, I didn't think the kitchen needed new paint. After twenty-seven years there was still a goodly portion of it on the walls, and if I may be so bold as to say, the scuff marks and chipped paint matched our table and chairs. I agonized for days about the upcoming painting until it dawned on me that here was the chance to get the new power paint roller the guys had been talking about. You know the one, a paint roller that plugs in. I believe this thing draws about 10 amps and it literally machine-guns the paint to the walls. This weapon will cover an entire wall in literally seconds. Your completion time is directly co-related to how fast you can roller blade from one end of the room to the other. Yes, I was pumped and I'm sure my enthusiasm did not go unnoticed by my wife; I sensed extra points coming up.

However, I was not allowed to buy the power paint roller. My wife's only reason was something about running with scissors; whatever that means. Consequently, we began the big job with nothing more exciting than paint brushes and a roller that did not plug in. As I layered the paint on the wall, I found myself thinking of golf. Indeed, the roller reminded me of a club, and I worked for a while on my swing, grooving it and really pounding the ball way-out-there. Then, it was my tennis backhand that got some much-needed work. All of this fun activity with a lowly paint roller made me realize that painting and decorating were not so bad after all. The paint was actually flying onto the walls.

Like most of the good times that I have enjoyed around the house, this one came to a sudden end. I looked over at my wife and I froze with fear and panic. It seems that my enthusiastic work ethic had gotten out of hand. Although she did not realize it as yet, her entire back had acquired all the markings of a speckled trout, albeit in a lovely avocado.

I was in deep trouble and my mind went into panic mode. Should I tell her the truth? That is what responsible grown-up adults do, but that route has gotten me into difficulty before. I briefly considered the Witness Protection Program but they had told me in the past not to call them again. It is kind of ironic, isn't it? A mafia hit man, who may or may not be in trouble, achieves free protection. However, an innocent man, who is in real danger because he has just speckled up his wife, is left to suffer and probably lose all of this year's, plus next year's points.

Luckily, the solution came to me before she caught on, and I can thank my past TV sports training for coming to my rescue. Waiting for my wife to face me, I accidentally "hip-checked" her into the wall; getting paint all over her. I then caught a lecture on being clumsy, but after all the injuries she has suffered while dancing with me, this body contact came as no surprise to her. Really, I have hip-checked her worse in the past.

All in all, the experience was a total success. My wife and I have never felt closer to each other, especially during the hip-check. There were some minor problems; we should have covered the furniture in the living room, as well as the kitchen. A window was left opened during the painting and my wife's car, carelessly parked in the driveway, now has a lovely metal-flake paint job in avocado. I'm sure that these things happen to active couples every day.

The above good deed was more than enough to qualify for the Dreamboat Husband Award, but anyone who knows me and my gift of generosity, will realize that I would not stop there. When you give an award, you must set the standard, and I next chose one of the toughest household tasks known to man. I did the laundry.

Before we begin my in-depth dissertation on doing the laundry, let me say a few words about my gallant involvement in household chores. Excuse me for being so brutally honest, but I have never shied away from contributing to the overall wellness of our happy home. The Young Male should not expect to rack up as many points as I do, and he may never qualify for the DHA, but by merely following along with the lesson, he cannot help but become a better person. I describe this phenomenon as such; "by brushing up against Superman, a small amount of heroism will rub off." I'm always available to be brushed up against. Let us continue on with the lecture.

We have nothing to fear except fear itself, and the unbleachables.

This wonderful old adage that I just recently made up perfectly depicts the household chore of doing the laundry. We do fear the unbleachables because we have not a clue as to what they are, what they look like, and where they reside in our house. We know that we have them because our wives discuss them all the time, and they appear on TV commercials during the hockey game.

Now, for the first time in the vast history of married life, husbands will fear no more; at least this one aspect of marriage. The marriage doctor has conquered the unbleachables and every other facet relating to laundry, otherwise known as the most feared of household chores. In this historic Primer lesson, I will pass along my success to my faithful followers.

Picture yourself sitting in the local sports bar, minding your own business and suddenly you get hit by an errant chicken wing. This happens more than one would think and if it doesn't happen by accident, someone will usually stand up and hurl one, just for the sake of doing it. The colour drains from your face, you begin to sweat uncontrollably, and your friends look at you like someone who has just taken a chair on death row. It is only a matter of time before you have to go home and face your wife. While she never wants to get close enough to check your breath for chicken wings, tonight she won't have to—the evidence is written all over your shirt.

Imagine this tragedy unfolding, and the wearer of the wing standing up and chortling, chortling in the face of terror because he knows that he can look fear in the face and chortle; chortle because he has conquered the previously unconquerable household chore, doing the laundry.

Before we can learn how to wash our clothes, there is one important step; finding the laundry room. This is done by simply following your wife downstairs. There is a visual hint that we must connect with laundry. This important clue is the load of dirty clothes in her arms. Do not follow her if she is taking a black plastic bag outside. This is called taking out the trash someplace, and we will cover that in another lesson.

Okay. You have found the room with the specialized machines, and your wife is ecstatic that you are even in this part of the house. After making sure that you are here to learn and you are not just lost, she begins to shout out instructions. Tune her out as per usual. For one thing, her way of doing laundry is complicated and time-consuming. Another reason for not listening is your inability as a married male to take instructions, or even to follow along carefully for any length of time. Just nod your head whenever she looks at you and also when there is a pause in her directives. Later, you will be doing the laundry alone as a surprise for her, and the Primer way is foolproof and much faster. You stand obediently beside her, until she is either finished doing the wash, or your legs become tired.

We now fast forward to a later date when you are prepared to surprise her with your newfound skill. You have a heap of dirty clothes on the floor and using your limited long term memory, you recall your wife saying something about sorting clothes by colours. I like to skip this step. It seems insignificant because she did not write it down for me. More importantly, if I can blend everything together in the washing machine, we can eliminate this confusing step altogether. This makes good sense to me. A family wearing all the same colour, or at least a close proximity, seems to be closer.

You were also told to sort by fabric types. Once again, you were given only verbal instructions, and although you recall exactly the different types of materials involved; nylon, rayon, argon, carbon, moron, and klingon—you draw a blank as to how to deal with them. Again, my own experience has shown me that this kind of sorting is unnecessary. I throw everything in and then address the individual needs as a whole.

For delicate hand-wash-only items, I scrub them lightly with a bar of mild hand soap, and then throw the entire bar in with the delicates. I like to dump in some of my wife's hair shampoo with conditioner; it gives your underclothes unbelievable body. You can really feel the softness and incredible manageability when you run your fingers through your underwear after the wash.

There is a spray-and-wash product that is meant for problem areas like food stains on your shirt. I believe that my directives were to spray each individual stain on every single garment. It is no wonder that there are not enough hours in the day for a housewife, my poor wife has been spraying chicken wing barbeque sauce her entire adult life. Go ahead and duct tape the spray trigger open and throw it in the washer.

For the rest of the clothes, do not be afraid to experiment. There are a myriad of detergents and bleaches on the market today that will do quite nicely. A good rule of thumb is; if the product is anywhere near the laundry facilities, it was meant to be used. Dump them all in.

There is always the question of how much laundry you can you put in the machine for one wash. If you have one of the fancier models with a hinged-lid on top, the answer is—when the lid is tough to close, you're full. Tough to close means that your body weight is required to close the lid. Hop up there and move around heavily until you feel that the lid is even with the top of the machine.

Actually, sitting on the washer serves a dual purpose, the aforementioned closing of the lid, and also because you have more than likely loaded it unevenly. Once you hit the fire-button, that baby is going to dance all over the basement. You will need to sit up there for an entire cycle. If you are a big man like me, you stand a good chance of keeping the washing machine in the general vicinity of your starting point.

Your preparation is done. You are sitting on top of a basement-bomb with 160 pounds of clothes and forty-five pounds of laundry products. You are pumped, quivering with anticipation, and we haven't even begun to add water. Isn't this fun?

Put on a hard hat. I prefer to use my patent-pending Dr. Murray Dick Laundry Helmet that will be available soon in fine local sports bars everywhere. You are in for a wild ride so secure the chin strap; there is the danger of landing on the hard cement floor, and also of rattling around in the overhead ceiling joists. The pre-game warm up is almost over. Reach up and grab onto a water pipe. With your free hand, start poking at the buttons on the washer control panel until you feel some movement underneath, and then hold on. You are doing the laundry the quick, easy, Primer way.

At some point in the cycle, all movement and vibration will come to a halt. Your first thought is that the laundry is complete, but be wary. The washing machine has many moods and will spring back to life at any time. If you feel the need to go to the bathroom, or you feel sick to your stomach, either pull the electrical plug and dismount, or use the handy laundry tub located conveniently for your use beside the washer.

Once the machine has come to a final rest, it is time to complete the household chore by ironing and drying. There are some clothing items that need ironing and fortunately my wife instructed me on these. Unfortunately, I wasn't listening again, so I just grab whatever will fit on the special board made exclusively for ironing. It is cleverly called the ironing board. We are now ready.

I prefer to wet iron. That is, I pull the clothes from the washer and slap them on the board. I plug in my iron, select the hottest setting to combine both ironing and drying, and away I go. I really don't know why this activity is called ironing; it should be called chasing wrinkles because that is basically what goes on. The wrinkle is always running ahead of your iron, but once in a while you catch one.

When you succeed in capturing a wrinkle under the iron, keep it there. You have just spent long minutes corralling it and this is no time to let it get away. For removing the actual wrinkle, a good rule of thumb is to count to thirty. There is going to be a lot of heat generated with this procedure, and it is a good idea to learn how to distinguish the difference between steam and smoke. Through trial and error, I found that when your eyes start to water and you can't breathe, it is time to move to another area.

Next, we will spend a few minutes discussing straight drying, without the ironing. I am quite sure that we have a drying machine, although I have never seen it in action. I like to go with the ever-popular green movement and air-dry my laundry. This is the environmentally friendly way to go, but I think you will agree that a fixed clothesline can be a problem to trim around when your wife is cutting the grass. I prefer to string the garments wherever—using any and all space in our yard.

In closing, let me advise the Young Male that laundry does not have to be a dull, household chore. A little experimentation will bring out the fun, and do not be afraid to go against the norm in your quest to help the wife in this endeavor.

Unfortunately, I have only been able to do the laundry once in our entire marriage. With my lucrative at-home woodworking business booming, and my ever-popular amateur marriage doctoring primer gaining notoriety, if not brisk sales, it's hard for me to find the time to help out these days. Strangely enough, my wife does not seem to mind, but I don't think that I will ever forget the one day I surprised her with my gift.

It was a beautiful spring day. I can still hear the birds chirping and see them roosting on some dress pants drying in our front-yard tree. The sun was shining brightly, softly kissing some blouses stretched out on the cement driveway, anchored down with stones gathered from the flower beds. The soft breeze seemed to whisper a wonderful melody as it rustled through a brassiere hung on the mailbox. It was one of those magical marriage moments that neither spouse ever forgets.

My wife returned home to this wonderful surprise. I watched her as she surveyed my gift to her. She looked all around; at her blouses on the ground, her bra on the mailbox, and she was speechless. There are no words at a time like this, only a cherished silence. She stared at me for a long time, giving me that look that I have come to know as my very own special look. She slowly turned, and went quietly into the house.

I think she went there to cry.

The Young Male should not expect to receive this same wonderful reception when he surprises his wife by doing the laundry. However, by starting small and working up to the major household chores, he will gain much needed expertise. And who knows, someday he may find himself walking down the aisle at the local sports bar, grabbing that special honourary pencil crayon and joining the ranks of the heroic— the winners of the coveted Dreamboat Husband Award. You too can become a heart-throb; the kind of man a woman dreams of.

The Young Male's Marriage Primer
Lesson Ten
Valentine's Day

Dr. Murray Dick

As the Young Male works his way through The Primer Curriculum, he encounters a wide variety of subjects and their various degrees of importance. We talked about the point system and communication; both extremely crucial aspects of successful married life. The student was also entertained and given a much needed break from his studies with a literary classic, *Agnes, the Canada Goose.* Up to this point, the lessons have been both manageable and positive.

Just reading the title of this lesson is enough to send chills and shivers down the backs of all men, both married and single. I believe I read somewhere that Valentine's Day was invented by a heartless, cold-blooded woman. She relished seeing men sweat, quiver with angst and anguish, and fall pathetically short when buying their wives or girlfriends suitable gifts. And quiver and shake they do, unable to cope with the pressures and anxieties brought on by this vile and dreaded day.

The shaking and quivering are over. *The Young Male's Marriage Primer* has never, and will never, back down from the tough issues, and Valentine's Day may be man's toughest quest to date. The problem is obvious; men know nothing about the gifts that women want on February the something, but they go ahead and buy these things anyway. Unfortunately, disaster is waiting when their significant others open these presents. The solution on how to educate males in purchasing these items was anything but apparent.

Before we get into the actual problem and the subsequent solution put forth by *The Primer*, I would like to address a couple of phrases associated with Valentine's Day. The Young Male may have possibly heard these spoken by this wife, but the average male has come to know and fear these expressions.

The first phrase is "You don't have to get me anything." This is the filthiest lie in the long history of marriage. This quote dates all the way back to the cave where the first wife grunted out this very same citation on the very first Valentine's Day. When Mr. Cave Man came home with nothing, he received the very first recorded head-trauma injury, inflicted with a blunt-edged club.

They all say it as if they mean it, but every woman on earth says it and doesn't mean it. For years, I heard this very thing, and for years, I brought nothing home. For years I took pleasure in the ensuing strip search after informing her that I bought her exactly what she had asked for. They say that strip searches are both invasive and degrading. Not in our house, I look forward to them. In the right hands, a proper strip search can be a wonderfully exciting experience. In looking back, it could have led to more intimate things if the searcher had not been so livid with rage. I do remember standing perfectly still until she got to a ticklish part. The phrase should be: "You don't have to get me anything. What's that? You didn't get me anything? Okay, up against the wall and spread 'em."

The other phrase that I would like to discuss is, "It's the thought that counts." Again we have an untruth. Let us say that you buy your Valentine's Day card like most married men do. You drive your cart past the greeting card section at the grocery store, and you pick one on the fly. You take it home, sign it quickly, and proudly give it to your wife. You have no idea that there are inconsiderate, thoughtless people who read cards and forget to put them back in their rightful places. "It's the thought that counts" does not hold much water when you have just given your wife a card intended for grandma, wishing her a speedy recovery from her most recent attack of gout. We will talk more about Valentine's Day cards later on in the lesson.

The applicable gifts on Valentine's Day are well known—lingerie, flowers, jewelry, and perfume—to name a few. The average married male does not do well shopping for these things because he knows absolutely nothing about them. We have already discussed the perils related to buying lingerie in an earlier lesson, but it bears repeating. I strongly suggest a hands-off policy when it comes to women's underwear and the reasons abound.

You buy some small, slinky underwear, the same style that all the popular girls are wearing in the magazines, but when your wife confronts you about this gift, you get questioned about your intentions. She keeps the skimpy present because she is too embarrassed to return it. If you purchase some really large underthings (they have the nerve to call them briefs), the kind that should accompany the card for grandma and her gout, this will raise a whole new set of troubles dealing with just how fat you think she is. Once again, I suggest a hands-off approach in dealing with women's underwear.

You would think that your wife might appreciate some fine jewelry, but this is not such a good idea. You purchase an expensive set of diamond earrings and the dog accidentally knocks them off your wife's dresser, shattering them all over the floor. When you go back to try to get a refund, you find that the van has pulled away and suddenly you are out thirty dollars. If you are going to shell out big bucks for fine jewelry, at least get a license plate number.

Women can always use a good quality perfume. They can use it as an air freshener at the cottage; they can use it to kill weeds in driveway cracks, and they can use it as a makeshift pepper spray to ward off physical assault.

I gave my wife a lovely fragrance one Valentine's Day and she casually remarked, "Should I decide to return this because I'm not worthy of such a fine gift, which hardware store should I go to?" I was speechless and shocked. I never knew that hardware stores sold fine quality scents and I have been searching these establishments ever since, but with no luck.

With all of these things in mind, I retreated to my workshop where the very roots of *The Primer* were born. In this safe haven, I mulled over the problem. The table saw droned beneath my hands for days on end as my mind searched and sought out a resolution.

One afternoon, I gazed at our brand new band saw and wished that my wife would accept a gift such as this potent, yet delicately balanced power tool. If only she could love and cherish something such as this, instead of forcing me to purchase a gift I knew nothing about—a gift prized only because it was associated with romance.

The answer came to me like a lightning bolt on a warm August evening. It was all so clear to me now; the solution to the Valentine's Day problem. Men were buying gifts in places out of their comfort zone and trying to be romantic. Men should be buying gifts in their comfort zone and presenting them romantically. These zones would include hardware stores, lumber yards, and leading power tool outlets everywhere. It really wouldn't matter what a women got as long as it was presented with a high degree of romance.

This colossal breakthrough in Valentine's Day gift-giving would change relationships forever. Men could now purchase things that they were familiar with. As an added bonus, if the female did not like her present, he would not have to take it back. The married male could keep it and play with it himself.

Once again, the raw power of *The Young Male's Marriage Primer* had been demonstrated and a completely new, cutting-edge marital technique had been theorized. To prove my new theory, The Romance Her until She Giggles Technique, I once again turned to a series of Primer Field Studies, conducted down at the local sports bar.

I chose as my subjects, married men who were having trouble dealing with Valentine's Day. In other words, I had my pick of the entire assemblage. To gain their confidence and get their cooperation, I reminded them of all the excellent counselling that I had given them over the years. When this didn't work, I offered free beer and wings to any volunteers.

Having thus gained their confidence and cooperation, I began my field studies. My first experiment was with a gentleman who confessed that his wife was less than ecstatic when Valentine's Day rolled around. In fact, both of them had given up on the celebration of this day completely. Her only wish was that they watch something other than the hockey game on that night. After some sensitive badgering on my part, I uncovered one of his favorite pastimes; he was an avid fisherman. I had found his comfort zone—the place where he would purchase her next treasured gift. All that was needed was the romantic presentation.

My patent-pending, revolutionary, Primer Romance Card accompanied her gift and reads as follows:

On opposite sides of the water we stand,
In the middle we long to meet.
And now when you wade through that river of love
You'll be dry right up past your seat.

My client was incredibly impressed and he said that his wife was speechless when she discovered her present to be hip-waders. She could find no words to convey the deep emotional thoughts that she was feeling for him. In fact, she was unable to speak to him for days. And it's no wonder. To the average layman, this Primer Romance Card is nothing more than a wonderfully romantic four-line sonnet; but it is so much more.

This lucky woman is conjuring up a lovely body of water, teeming with lively fish, possibly brook trout, or large mouth bass. As she eagerly watches her husband across the way, she cannot help but notice how her new hip-waders caress her almost-nude lower torso, right down to her sweat socks. She hears the murmur of insects; she witnesses the beauty of the elusive firefly, usually invisible during broad daylight. Suddenly, the tranquility is shattered by the call of the Canada goose, "Honk, Honk, Honkity Honk." She glances up to catch a brief glimpse of the muscular leader, and oh my! What a "hunka', hunka', burning goose" he is.

She gracefully enters the water. The little waves lapping at her body, making romantic little lapping noises. As she reaches the middle, she glances across at her husband, her brave knight in shining armor, her Sir Galahad, who is bravely trying to free his foot from a rock crevice. This kind of stuff will romance the giggles out of a woman. I invented this technique, and even I get goose bumps when I think of it.

Flushed with success, I was tempted to incorporate The Romance Card technique into *The Primer*, but the Valentine's Day problem was rampant and universal in its nature. (It was all across our little town.) I decided that further experimentation was needed before releasing this powerful new marriage doctoring tool as an actual lesson.

For my next field study, I chose a patient named Wilbur. He is a well known gardener who displays an immaculate lawn each summer, and is constantly talking about the value and benefit of a groomed landscape.

As a matter of fact, Wilbur talks to the point of alienating most of the guys down at the local sports bar. All they know is that someone cuts the grass—they care little about whom, why, when, or how.

Wilbur was a prime candidate for purchasing gifts inside his comfort zone. He knew absolutely nothing about the usual Valentine's Day gifts. What he did know, was weed-whackers.

Wilbur could be easily fooled by perfumes, women's clothes, and the like, but he possessed an extensive knowledge of weed-whackers. All you had to do was breach the subject of the new one that he had his eye on, and away he'd go—commenting on how this one had auto-load, with state-of-the-art Teflon string (the very same string developed for use on the space shuttle flights), and a comfortable easy-grip handle. He would rave about the tool's ability to slice through a small sapling, if ever the need arose, and let's not forget the thirty month money-back guarantee, should it fall apart.

All these features sounded very nice, especially if you are a weed-whacker aficionado, but Wilbur had no faith in his wife's acceptance of such a valuable gift. Using the special technique that I had invented for just such an occasion, I unleashed the power of *The Primer* in the form of the following Primer Romance Card. This accompanied her lovely Valentine's Day present:

> *See the garden we share lit by stars from above,*
> *Hark the dawn; now it glistens in dew.*
> *When doubt, lies, and weeds try to strangle our path,*
> *My darling, I'll go 'whacking' with you.*

Weed-whacker men are commonly known as some of the toughest people on earth—daily subjecting their bodies to severe injury from flying debris and potential scratches from the numerous cats that they flush out of flowerbeds. Wilbur even compares it to rodeo bull riding in the danger aspects; going on to say that whacking might be more hazardous because bull riders do not have to wear hearing protection.

At any rate, Wilbur broke down and wept when he read The Primer Romance Card. He cried like a baby. His wife, like the hip-wader woman, was equally enthralled and moved beyond words for days. Wilbur himself has become a changed man. He no longer speaks of weed-whackers in technical jargon; his speech has become laced with romantic metaphors which has turned his yard maintenance program into an art form.

It is no longer a weed-whacker, but his divining rod; uniting him with Mother Earth. The high pitch drone, that previously penetrated even the most efficient hearing protection, has now become their song. These days, when the couple walks through the neighbourhood and the distant, mournful sound of a weed-whacker catches his ear; his hand reaches for, and grasps, that of his wonderfully lucky wife.

Life has become newer, slower, and more laid-back for Wilbur since *The Primer* revitalized his marriage. He now has this message for the guys down at the local sports bar. "Life is too precious to speed through, you have to stop and smell the two-cycle oil-gas mixture." This is a lovely, touching testimony from a gratified client, showing once again the raw, natural power of *The Young Male's Marriage Primer*.

There was one last test to conduct before my patent-pending marriage technique, The Primer Romance Card, could be incorporated into the actual lessons. It would be a tough test, but as you know, my incredible success in amateur marriage doctoring has not been achieved by shying away from problem situations. I had been toying with the idea of altering my revolutionary, cutting-edge technique of comfort-zone shopping just slightly enough to include the traditional Valentine's Day gifts.

I decided to make my own perfume in my workshop, using wood glue and walnut-wood sawdust. The combination of presenting my wife with an old fashioned Valentine's Day gift and the accompanying Primer Romance Card, would more than make up for pre-Primer years—when my presents could best be described as so-so.

After much trial and error, and a whole lot of sneezing and coughing, I had developed a wonderful fragrance that I believe captured the atmosphere of the shop, and also depicted the deep emotional feelings I held for my wife. Wally was visibly excited over this new venture and suggested that we market the scent under the name Eau de Walnut. He even went so far as to design a few labels, including such descriptions as; "a remarkably subtle, yet overpowering fragrance—capturing the smell of the woods and all the animals therein, both alive and dead." Wally, ever the safety advocate, felt compelled to add this disclaimer on the label. "Keep away from small children and pets; do not breathe in contents of vial. Contact with eyes will cause mild to severe retinal damage instantly. If accidental contact occurs, rinse eye with cleaning solvents only—using water will activate the wood glue and seal your eye shut forever."

There have been moments during the development of *The Primer* when all the hard work on my part has been worthwhile. Such was the case last Valentine's Day when I presented my lovely wife with her charming perfume present and accompanying Primer Romance Card.

She hesitantly opened the card and read its contents. She was awestruck with its romantic overtones and reluctantly, with my coaxing, opened her little perfume prize package. As she pried the lid off, the lovely fragrance caressed her nasal cavities and she was overcome with emotion—overcome to the point of sneezing, coughing, heaving, retching, and grabbing a spoon to scrape her tongue. Never, in all my years as an amateur marriage doctor, have I seen a woman so moved from a single act of romantic kindness. Never have I watched a woman shake and heave as my lucky wife did from the passion and sentiment that I incorporated into this gift.

She slowly returned to the kitchen table, remained completely silent, and gave me that special look—a look reserved for me only, a look that I have come to know and love during our past forty-seven years of marriage. Turning, she unsteadily walked down to the bedroom, careening off the walls on the way.

The Primer Romance Card read:
This gift from the heart on this special of days,
Proves my unbridled love for thee.
I know that you'll still take my old breath away.
When you smell like a large walnut tree.

I believe that she went down there to cry.
Good luck on Valentine's Day to married males everywhere.

The Young Male's Marriage Primer
Lesson Eleven
Magical Vacation Moments

Dr. Murray Dick

The main emphasis of *The Young Male's Marriage Primer* is preparing the newlywed for a successful home life. However, the versatility that I have embedded in this manual will allow the student to deal with life, and its many facets—different avenues if you will. The Young Male must be prepared to adapt to these diverse environments if he wishes to gain the high level of success that I have achieved in my own marriage of thirty-five years.

I cannot count the number of times that young people have come up to me and said, "Gee, Dr. Murray Dick, you are always so focused, so totally dedicated, and so extremely sensitive to your entire family's needs, even while you are on vacation far away from home. How do you do it?"

My answer is simple and from the heart. It is a wonderful old adage that I just recently made up, "Good husbandry never takes a holiday, even while on holidays." I have enjoyed many wonderful family vacations throughout the years—vacations that have bonded our family into the tightly knit unit that defines us.

The Young Male will be venturing forth on his own vacations with his wife, and eventually their young children will be joining them. It is a wise man who appreciates these moments because all too soon the kids have grown up and are out on their own. I remember the good times, the family outings, but I also recall that sad moment when my own two daughters felt that maybe they would like to spend time with their own friends, and that perhaps Dad just wasn't cool enough. I believe my daughters were five and three years of age at the time. Even though this can be a painful experience, especially for a family as close as our own, I took heart in the fact that I had done my job as an unselfish parent. Although they were now busy with their own lives, I still have many grand memories to comfort me in my twilight years that loom ahead. They grow up so fast, don't they?

If the student has learned his lessons well, he is becoming rather proficient in the basics of marriage survival as covered in previous chapters. However, he must branch out. The Young Male must extend his range of expertise in marital achievements to those times when it is not as easy to be generous; when the temptations of selfishness are all too strong. One of the times when he must put aside his own wants and needs, and put his family first, is while on vacation.

Once again, I will be utilizing one of *The Primer's* most powerful techniques, Teaching by Example. I will be presenting two glorious vacations for the student to study. Each holiday trip was chosen for its own specific qualities, but prevalent in both examples is the essence of *The Primer's* main focus—teaching, leadership, heroism, and all encompassing generosity.

The first holiday presented is one that we spent with my brother-in-law Wally and his family. Just the mere fact that Wally would take time off from his career as an out-of-work master plumber speaks volumes of his devotion to the needs of others. He displays an uncanny sense of leadership and thoughtfulness while on vacation. Wally is a wonderfully dedicated family man, and it was a privilege to spend some quality time with him away from the local sports bar.

To witness Wally at the cottage is inspiring. His safety standards are legendary. How many senseless tragedies will it take to convince people that safety never takes a holiday? We have all seen boaters flying down the lake, wearing no personal floatation devices—an accident waiting to happen. A common excuse is, "Well, I just forgot." This cannot happen with Wally. He dons his lifejacket before he makes the drive up to the cottage. While most men would consider it uncomfortable to wear a seat belt along with a bulky life-preserver, Wally never hesitates to buckle up for safety. Perhaps he says it best; "It gives me added confidence knowing that if I drive erratically along deep rivers, I won't perish, at least not by drowning." Many holiday travellers talk safety, my brother-in-law actually lives it.

You will not find many people as well suited for the rugged north as Wally, whose past training includes wilderness guiding and some basic pioneering. The pioneering experience comes from having the first house in a subdivision located in a rugged part of town, enduring many months of hardship and suffering, not unlike the early homesteaders. The similarities between Wally and the early pioneers are uncanny; neither had sidewalks in front of their homes for the first few months. In addition, they both endured months of mud before a sod-lawn was laid, and I'm quite sure that the pioneers also moved into their log cabins before their basements were finished.

Wally's credentials as a guide are impeccable. As a young lad, he spent a partial summer holiday working as a clerk down at the local supermarket. If you know Wally, it comes as no surprise that he possessed the imagination, and the drive, to memorize the whereabouts of every single product in the entire store. Even today, no one can come close to beating him at "stump the bag-boy." I would trust my life with Wally in the produce section of any grocery store.

We did not travel very far in our journey to the cottage before Wally's heroism first surfaced. Our pioneer scout spotted a man calling for help from his car and with absolutely no thought concerning his own personal well-being, Wally pulled the man to safety through the partially opened window. In retrospect, I guess we should have realized that people have to yell out of their windows when ordering an apple fritter at a doughnut shop drive-thru. Just the same, this act showcased Wally's willingness to intervene in a potentially dangerous situation. After the victim's children stopped crying, we bought lunch for his entire family and we continued on our way. Incidentally, I began to understand why Wally wore his life jacket for the whole vacation; it saved him from serious injury when the man's wife punched him repeatedly in the chest.

You have to see Wally at the cottage to appreciate the effort he puts into his life as a pioneer guide. It is not just family that he includes in his camp activities, but perfect strangers as well. Everyone at the resort, at some point in their stay, will be touched by his friendliness and social habits—whether they like it or not. There is an old stereotype of the married male who goes on vacation and just sits around his cottage drinking beer. Not so with Wally. He will go to a different cottage, introduce himself, and sit around their cabin, drinking their beer. Wally's visits are not the hit-and-run type where you barely get to know someone. No, he will stay for hours, until he's either called home for lunch, or the beer runs out. Wally calls this interaction his camp-meeting routine. I have seen Wally hold four or five camp meetings in a single afternoon. Sometimes, as he is walking home from the last meeting, he accidentally falls in the lake, and once again, I am reminded of why he wears his lifejacket twenty-four hours a day while on vacation.

On this particular holiday, Wally demonstrated his leadership skills in a brilliant display of pioneer craftsmanship. He gathered all of the camp children together and taught them how to make a birch bark canoe. The kids embraced the history behind this remarkable boat as Wally recalled stories of the fur trappers of Upper Canada who could not afford an outboard motor. These ingenious people were forced to make their own watercraft, and they became known as "courtesy-de-bois"—a French Canadian term with a literal meaning of "boys who make boats with no motors, in a polite sort of way." Upon completion of their own birch bark canoe, Wally even promised the kids a brief lesson on how to trap a chipmunk, tan the hide, and trade the pelt for some flour and bacon down at the local general store.

The first order of business in making this type of canoe is, of course, securing large amounts of birch bark. With Wally marking the proper trees in advance, the young group went about stripping the bark off every birch tree within two miles of camp. Once gathered, the bark was then applied to each and every cottage rental boat, using a staple gun. Unfortunately, the class had to be disbanded when an irate cottager discovered that his rubber dinghy had been converted into a birch bark canoe. He then threw Wally into the lake. Once again, the importance of wearing a lifejacket at all times was brought to mind and sadly, the chipmunk trapping seminar was never held. It is no wonder that the old trappers never used rubber dinghies to make their canoes; they only last a few minutes before sinking.

Wally was undeterred, and his next order of business was to hold survival training for the camp youth. He has championed the art of survival under harsh conditions ever since he was marooned in his basement during a blackout. If you remember, this was an unfinished basement, so there were no amenities such as a beer fridge for sustenance, or a TV to pass away the lonely hours, until he found his way to the stairs. For days, it was just him and the damp, clammy cement walls. Just as a side note, Wally has written a pamphlet on this type of tragedy called, "Surviving the Terror of an Unfinished, Unlit Basement." His dream is to ensure that everyone in town has a copy of this lifesaving literature in their basement. Someone questioned the value of having a pamphlet in your basement if you cannot see to read it. Wally is looking into publishing it in Braille.

Let's get back to the survival training. The plan was to blindfold all the children and lead them off into the woods. The kids would be supplied with a few doughnuts and a bottle of water; the clothes on their backs would be their only shelter. The use of a compass was considered cheating. The young survivalists were to find their way back to camp and the safety of their cabins, using only the stars, and the constant honking of the panic button on Wally's truck. (Honk! Honk! Honkity, Honk!) I think that the children would have benefited greatly from this experience had not some adults got wind of it, and threw Wally into the lake again—just for thinking up such a plan.

We never ventured out on the lake to fish. The entire fleet of camp boats had been hauled out of the water for some sort of maintenance. Therefore, Wally decided to conduct a class on dry-land casting. He assembled a few kids who were able to sneak out of their cottages, and he began to teach them how to cast great distances, getting the bait 'way out there where the big ones swim. Because he is so safety conscious, Wally gave each youth a goalie mask for protection against any errant casts. While this did stop the hook from injuring a little boy on one of Wally's wild throws, it did not stop the bait from penetrating the mask. We were surprised to learn that a dew worm, traveling close to ninety miles per hour, can actually become glued to a face. As the little boy ran home crying, Wally sensed the inevitable and jumped into the lake.

There was a somber note to our vacation. One day, as Wally was having a nap on the dock, he was attacked and bitten by a swarm of mosquitoes, or so we think. He is a very sound sleeper which allowed the bugs to gnaw on him for quite awhile. He finally woke up due the incredible pain, and also because he was hungry. Wally swore up and down that he was attacked by marauding chipmunks. He claimed that while they can be quite cute when alone, in a mob atmosphere they have been known to become vicious.

I asked him if this could have been one of his beer-induced nightmares that he has been known to have from time to time. He once told me that after a night at the local sports bar, he had dreamt that a giant nimbus cloud was devouring him, only later to discover that his wife had administered his anti-snoring pillow during the night.

If it was the chipmunks, this went against everything we knew about these cute little forest creatures. We went down to the general store and asked some of the older locals if there was any truth to attacking chipmunks. One of them leaned back in his rocking chair and said that he had heard about us and the talk about a chipmunk trapping seminar. The chipmunks probably got wind of it too. He went on to add that they were extremely smart animals, especially around here, and that they had probably put out a hit on the guy wearing a lifejacket all day long. He also said that, because Wally resembled a peanut—a really big peanut—it would require about thirty or forty chipmunks to get him home; even after whittling him down to a manageable size.

The local guy recommended that we protect ourselves for the duration of our stay, suggesting that we purchase an authentic chipmunk-repellent hat, guaranteed to ward off the most vicious of forest critters. Luckily, he had two for sale.

As the old codger explained it, "Chipmunks have only one natural predator, the squirrel. If you wear this hat with a genuine squirrel tail on it, they will give you a wide berth."

The hat reminded me of the old coonskin cap that "Daniel Crockett" made famous years ago, but these were fifty dollars apiece, and I don't remember Daniel coughing up that much money.

The old man stated that Wally was now a marked man. He should wear the hat backwards to get maximum tail protection on his well-bitten and gnawed face. We left these men to their discussions and joke-telling (we could hear laughter all the way down the road), and the rest of the week we wore our chipmunk protection. Wally found the tail in his face somewhat difficult at first, but eventually he became used to it; even going to camp meetings and drinking around the tail. The good news is that there were no more chipmunk attacks.

All-in-all, it was a very pleasurable vacation. Wally and I had seven wonderful days at the lake, our wives had seven wonderful days shopping at the local mall, and the children of the camp went home with memories to last a lifetime. Wally taught me that the names of the local wildlife were derived from the native language. The loon, roughly translated, means "some kind of big goose with spots." The beaver is translated as "splashing tailgate," and the word chipmunk means "little jaws of death."

We were not able to go for a boat ride, but Wally said that he swam more than in past years, which is good. He wore his chipmunk-repellent hat home just to be on the safe side. However, his wife wouldn't let him drive with a dead squirrel's tail hanging in his face.

I do hope that the Young Male can see how leadership, heroism, and true pioneering spirit can enhance a holiday, not just for yourself, but also for the people around you. Wally could have sat back and enjoyed the vacation, but his willingness to give made him reach out; taking the initiative to meet the many new faces in their own cabins, and enjoying their hospitality. He also spent quality time with the young campers to ensure that the next generation is wise in the way of our pioneering ancestors. He is a true friend and a wonderful brother-in-law.

The final example that I would like to present to the Young Male is taken from my own personal vault of vacations. As previously mentioned, we had many fine outings as a family unit, but for this lesson I have chosen one involving just my wife and me. We planned a trip to the west coast of Canada from our small rural town in southwest Ontario. The purpose of the journey was to visit the many fine power tool stores in Vancouver, British Columbia. We also planned to visit some of my wife's relatives whom she had not seen in twenty years, if we had the time.

I have divided each segment into a magical moment, demonstrating to the student how I maintain my incredible sensitivity, to not only my wife, but to fellow travellers along the way. The title of the journey could well be called, "On the Trail of the Wild Caribou," which will become obvious as the story unfolds. Remember Young Males, good husbandry never takes a holiday, even when on holidays.

Dr. Murray Dick's Magical Vacation Moment: Number One

The first morning dawns bright and clear. I have been driving along for several hours when I indicate to my wife that the truck was steering a little loosely, and perhaps our vacation gear in the back was improperly stowed. (I had been unable to help load the truck the day before because of a prior commitment at the local sports bar.) I casually mentioned that perhaps her suitcase with its three-hundred pounds of cosmetics would help the weight distribution if it were strapped to the hood of the truck.

My wife immediately replied, "Well, I put the three-hundred pound suitcase on my side of the truck and I hoped that its weight, combined with mine, might counter-balance the driver. Obviously, based on the severe tilt of the truck, I was wrong. Do the tires on your side have any air left in them?"

This magical vacation moment highlights my patented marriage technique, Communicating for Problem Solving. The steering dilemma seemed to clear itself up without any adjustment and we continued on our wonderful journey, albeit with less talking and a mental note to rotate the tires at every stop.

Dr. Murray Dick's Magical Vacation Moment: Number Two

I believe it was in the rugged wilderness north of Toronto, when I suggested to my wife that we play a rousing game of "name that road kill." This fun, but challenging contest, had entertained our family on many vacations, and although my wife refused to participate, I was busily calling out various species of unfortunate wildlife—even getting the odd one correct. I spotted a sure game winner and after yelling out, "wild caribou," I stopped the truck for a snapshot of the prize.

Although I was obviously mistaken, my wife still insisted on taking a picture. Several weeks after we returned home, I discovered a life-sized poster hanging up at the local sports bar. It was me, standing on the side of the road, holding up a large piece of truck tire. Wally said that it was an honest mistake, and that it actually looked like a wild caribou after he drew on some antlers.

Dr. Murray Dick's Magical Vacation Moment: Number Three

I believe we were in Northern Ontario, or perhaps it was Manitoba, or Saskatchewan. Who knows, it might even have been Newfoundland. At any rate, we were there for a week and if I knew where it was, I would not have been lost. Yes, I was lost, and for a good reason. A few years ago, my brother-in-law Wally discovered a conspiracy plot involving the roadmap industry. He went undercover as a tourist information ranger and his findings support the theory that faulty maps are routinely sold to encourage the traveller to purchase another map, and so on. Since that time, I have relied solely on my trusty Boy Scout compass for navigation, and I can proudly boast that a week of being lost is not too bad by my standards.

It was during this tenure that my wife and I had one of those wonderful marital conversations that all strong unions enjoy from time to time. I present this dialogue to show the Young Male that the bonds of marriage are made stronger through vocal interaction.

"Gee dear," I began. "Isn't this northern scenery the most beautiful that you have ever seen. It's so dense and green, with the next scene blending into the vista from before. I'm feeling a sense of 'déjà vu' every now and then, how about you?"

My wife replied, "It's not 'déjà vu'. Two days ago, you got us stuck between two big rocks. It's the same trees from yesterday, that's the same porcupine sitting on the hood, and there goes the same fur trapper—walking by us again and laughing his butt off."

I continued, "Well, we are getting good gas mileage. It's a good job that we put your quilting stuff in our truck survival kit—you're going to have that blanket completed in a few days."

She replied, "There's one other thing that I should have put in the kit—a responsible adult."

It takes time and effort to build this kind of rapport between two loving people. A relationship can only get stronger when a wonderful husband, like me, uses sensitivity and calm during a crisis situation.

The time spent stuck between two big rocks need not put undue stress on a marriage. I know this for a fact; it happens to me quite a lot.

Here is a little bit of irony. I actually have one of those on-board navigational systems, but I have never used it because I lost the instructions. I believe it is called "Lost Star," and during our wilderness journey between the two rocks, they actually called me to tell me that their entire company was watching our progress, or lack thereof.

The nice lady said that their office had a pool going and the choices were that I was either in a float plane, hot-air balloon, or I was in a sled pulled by reindeer. I told her that I was stuck between two big rocks, and I asked if she could send a tow truck. She replied that we happened to be six-hundred miles from the nearest gravel road, but if I remained there until the tow-helicopter returned, they would send it up.

Well, they never did send their tow-helicopter, but luckily, a deluge of rain washed us free of the rocks and we were finally on our way—with a lot worse gas mileage, I might add. For the next few days, the Lost Star lady would call, giggle at me and call me Waldo, which I believe was "Christopher Columbia's" middle name. I thank her for that.

There is a bright side to this scenic Northern Ontario, or Manitoba, or Eastern Quebec leg of our trip. I truly believe that I actually saw the boat launch used in the movie Deliverance, and enjoyed a pleasant lunch there with the locals. My wife, being not hungry during the period we were lost, stayed in the truck. It's funny, for the rest of the trip she refused to listen to any of my banjo music tapes. I also believe that I saw a wild mother caribou and her baby calf up there. Yes, I am quite sure that I did.

Dr. Murray Dick's Magical Vacation Moment: Number Four

Ah the prairies, in all their glorious simplicity, the unbroken silence, the never-ending ribbon of empty asphalt highway stretching to the far-off horizon that seems ever-unreachable in this realm of big-sky country—a never-ending, glorious, silent journey.

As I drove through this wheat-field wonderland, I turned to my slightly-dozing wife and philosophized. "You know dear, if you recline your seat somewhat and close your eyes, you can actually visualize the vast herds of wild caribou that once filled this great land in an earlier time. The miles just seem to whiz by when I do this; see if it works for you also." This seemed to jolt my wife awake and she insisted on driving, so I could continue to visualize from the passenger seat. She's a wonderful, caring lady, and also an accomplished speller. You don't often find a combination like that in a woman; I think I'll keep her.

I urge the young married males to share these types of experiences with their wives, no matter how insignificant they may seem. Magic moments such as these not only get your wife's attention, but bring you closer as you both travel down life's highway, visualizing great things together. I used this experience to generate my patented, state-of-the-art marriage saving technique, Sharing Your Driving Visions with Those You Love and Vice Versa.

Dr. Murray Dick's Magical Vacation Moment: Number Five

Calgary was our next stop, home of the famous Stampede—the largest outdoor exhibition of its kind in the world. While watching the bull riders, it suddenly struck me that I had much in common with these heroic athletes. During my high school days, I was also a rider. I had made the second string bicycle team. I would have advanced further if I had not sacrificed speed for proper safety procedures, such as signaling as I went around a banked curve, and pulling over to the right to allow faster bikes to pass. To this day, I still maintain that the Olympic cycling venue would be a much safer sport if they adopted my safety-first bicycle riding techniques.

At any rate, I told my wife that I was going backstage to talk to the bull riders. I wanted to share my riding experiences and ask if anyone needed some marriage doctoring help. My wife didn't think that this was such a great idea, but I reminded her of my uncanny ability to blend in during any situation. I have never practiced, or abused, my ability to mingle as an unfair advantage; it is just something that comes naturally to me.

The first thing that happened backstage was that I got bull stuff all over my sandals. In fact, it splattered over the top of my knee-high socks. Slipping, I "fouled" my new Hawaiian shirt and my stylish Gucci traveling shorts. I was then escorted from the backstage area, and after being denied entrance to the grandstand area (I didn't smell too good), I went to the parking lot and changed clothes beside my truck.

I have since gained a better understanding of the talents displayed by these fearless bull riders, for their ability to stay on for eight seconds, and also their agility in walking around bull stuff. I still believe that I could have been a credible bull rider, if not for my deathly fear of all farm animals, and also being prone to injury. (I tend to bruise just watering the lawn.)

Dr. Murray Dick's Magical Vacation Moment: Number Six

The magnificent Rockies: There is no lesson here, just the humbling aura of the mountains. One cannot help but ponder on the genius and hard work involved in the mapping and actual building of these treacherous tunnels in a time long ago—long before there were so many Tim Horton's doughnut shops.

Dr. Murray Dick's Magical Vacation Moment: Number Seven

This magic vacation moment is a wonderful example of my Putting Others Ahead of Yourself technique, and will show the Young Male how we should never take a holiday from this. Since publishing *The Primer*, I actually feel a responsibility to my fellowman to share my sensitivity and warmth.

I believe it was somewhere in British Columbia, that we decided to stay at a plush resort and dine in their expensive restaurant. This was a reward for having a safe trip through the mountains and also for driving one day in a row without getting lost. It was in this splashy, somewhat crowded dining area, that I arose and unselfishly yelled out, "I just had the wild caribou entrée, does anyone have to use the rest room before I go in there?"

Many thankful patrons raced to the facilities, even women for some reason. A few others fled the building entirely. I just knew that I had made the right decision in putting others first—even at my own unbelievable discomfort. My wife's reaction was typical. In past times such as this, similar benevolent behaviour on my part had left her speechless. She could find no words to convey her emotions. She put her napkin over her head, her face in her hands, and she went out to the truck. I truly believe that she went out there to cry.

This was not the end of our British Columbia experience. The resort that we stayed at was a five star, or so they said. It had all kinds of amenities—two swimming pools, a spa, a massage room, and various pubs (although it had no local sports bar). With all of these frills, you can imagine my surprise when we checked into our room and found that the bathroom had no ceiling exhaust-fan. For the most part, this was a non-issue; but the morning after our dining room meal, I called out to my wife from the bathroom, "Honey, have I ever had wild caribou before?"

She replied, "No, I would have remembered it, trust me."

At 8:30 A.M., I crawled over to the phone and called the restaurant desk and inquired, "Your wild caribou—exactly what are you feeding them these days?"

At 9:30 A.M., the entire staff of cleaning ladies set up picket lines at either end of our hallway.

At 9:31 A.M., my wife was sworn into their union.

At 10:00 A.M., I yelled down to the end of the hallway. "You know, this entire senseless tragedy could have been avoided with the proper installation of a ceiling exhaust-fan."

A cleaning lady yelled back, "Mister, they don't make 'em that big."

After packing all our belongings by myself, I found my wife in the truck, waiting patiently to continue our binding trip.

Dr. Murray Dick's Magical Vacation Moment: Number Eight

Mile Zero on the Trans Canada Highway is on the west end of Vancouver Island. We had finally made it. As I dipped my big toe in the waters of the vast Pacific Ocean, a large object caught my eye to my right. Yelling "wild caribou," I raced along the water's edge to get a picture of this beach kill. Once again, my eyes had deceived me. Once again, a life-sized poster of me hangs in the local sports bar; this time holding up a large piece of driftwood. Unfortunately, I was nabbed by an undercover beach ranger for loading park property into the back of my truck. After laughing at him and trying to escape, I spent the next week in jail while my wife scurried around trying to raise the twenty-dollar bail, doing some shopping, and visiting her close relatives.

Murray Dick's Magical Vacation Moment: Number Nine

We drove back through the mountains, eventually reaching Jasper Park, Alberta. There were numerous signs warning of the protected wildlife crossing the road. I spotted some movement in the bush and I yelled "wild caribou." After stopping the truck and sneaking soundlessly into the dense cover, I accidentally snapped a picture of a large beefy man from Manitoba using the forest.

I raced back to the truck and I answered my wife's query with, "Yes, it was a big one." We pressed on, speeding up after my wife informed me that my little reindeer friend was gaining on us, even while pulling up his pants.

This last, full-sized poster caused quite a buzz at the local sports bar, even after the drawn on antlers. My brother-in-law Wally said that the picture shows a study of contrasting looks; one of fear, such as a wild caribou caught in headlights, and the other, a vicious carnivore-like animal. The large beefy man from Manitoba seems to be looking at something that he would like to slowly and painfully kill. Only Wally, a dabbler in psychiatry, would view something this deeply.

Dr. Murray Dick's Magical Vacation Moment Summary

I think that the Young Male can now get a sense of what needs to be done to continue his education regarding good husbandry, even during family fun times. It is not easy putting others first all the time, but the rewards are worth it for every one involved, and you will feel good about yourself.

As a footnote to the magic vacation moments, let me assure the readers that I have made every attempt to contact the large beefy man from Manitoba, even posting his picture on the internet in an effort to identify him, and also apologize for taking his photo with his pants down around his ankles. Perhaps the antlers, which Wally drew on the picture, make recognition impossible. Sadly, he has not contacted me as yet. I believe that I have gone the extra mile in this endeavour and I will continue to post his picture and accompanying apology. Some day he will see it and more than likely thank me.

One final thought Young Males, the true measure of a successful vacation is the gratitude and sheer exhilaration that you bring to your loved ones. When asked if this vacation had memories to last a lifetime, my wife replied, "Oh yeah, at least."

Good husbandry never takes a holiday, even while on holidays.

The Young Male's Marriage Primer
Lesson Twelve
The Eating Habits of the Married Male
and also
Buffet Tactics

Dr. Murray Dick

Scientists have recently discovered, through numerous archeology digs, that early cave man was a ravenous meat-eater. Cave wall paintings show great hunters with mammoth and giant sloth grease all over their faces and shirts. These real men are surrounded by hordes of women—not the big-boned ones with nice personalities, but the choice, prime females. Skeletal remains confirm this data; vast multitudes of cave girls lying next to muscular he-men who have food stains all over their 'skins.' These extraordinary findings confirm, beyond a shadow of a doubt, that nature assures the survival of a species by showing the females that the greatest hunters are the ones with food all over themselves.

A leading archeologist scientist, tops in his field

This startling new discovery in the world of archeology science should finally put an end to the debate of why married males are messy eaters. For years, we have been led to believe that we spilled food all over ourselves because we were sloppy, but all the while, we were just displaying our ability to provide for a potential family. It is nature's way. Just as a side note, the study goes on to say that a few male skeletons were found buried without any female companions. Traces of spinach were found in their teeth.

Let me point out that this wasn't just any old scientist doing the research, but a leading scientist who, as anyone can plainly see, is also tops in his field. The exploration was commissioned by a major spare ribs company here in Upper Canada, and if you can't trust the spare ribs people, who can you trust?

I can almost hear two cave women talking outside their grotto. "Gee, Marlene, look at the mammoth grease all over Murray Dick's face. He has it all the way up over his broad, sloping forehead, and all the way down his hairy, swarthy back. It practically covers his saber-tooth tiger tee shirt. He must be a great provider. I wish that I hadn't chosen Wally for a mate. Maybe I'll go and line up with the other prime women for Murray Dick."

This will not be the only pure science made available here, as once again, I turn to my brother-in-law Wally who, as you know, likes to dabble in psychiatry. Although Wally did not agree with the two cave girls for some unknown reason, he has branched out to tackle the age-old problem of the eating habits of married men. He has two wonderfully sensitive books in the works; *You Are What You Eat, You Wear What You Eat*, and also, the soon-to-be classic, *You Are What You Eat, Please Pass the Butt Chops.* These books are more like pamphlets—only two or three pages long, but they are an insightful look into this fascinating topic.

Your eating habits have not changed since your marriage. The only thing that has changed is the how they are perceived. For example, the woman who raised you, and the woman you married, have vastly different perceptions of the way you eat. Your mother always referred to you as a hearty, aggressive eater, and when your food went awry on its way to your mouth, she would chuckle, wipe the mashed potatoes from her glasses, shake her head and mutter, "That's my boy."

However, your mother is not sitting across from you these days. It is a different woman with a completely different attitude towards your eating habits. She's not looking at a hearty, aggressive eater. No, she's looking at you with cold, stark eyes as the food flies around. She's looking at a pig with a fork.

You try to explain to her that a lot of the food-flinging is safety related. For example, eating meatballs can be extremely hazardous to the entire family, especially the young ones. When you come down on a meatball with your fork, there is a slim probability that you are going to hit it square on, resulting in a perfect meatball spear. Chances are, the fork is going to strike either side, turning that round chunk of meat into a dangerous projectile, propelling it in one of two directions.

Forgive me for caring about my children, but their safety is paramount to me. I always aim for the safety side of the meatball, and I am proud to say that in all my years as a father, I have never struck one of my children in the eye with a meatball. Okay, maybe the chin or the ear—but never the eye. I have, however, sacrificed myself and worn many a meatball. I've worn them on my shirt, down my shirt, in my shirt pocket, and so on, and so on. I've worn meatballs at home, in restaurants, at dinner parties, at lumberyard opening galas, and so on, and so on.

The average married male is constantly being bombarded with confusing information. If it is quite acceptable to eat pizza without utensils, you figure that all Italian food falls into this category. Try digging into a plate of lasagna with your bare hands at a church social and watch your wife's reaction. Were these two dishes not invented by the same Italian chef? The married male can learn, but he needs precise directions, and while you are giving him these instructions make sure they are simple.

Your children's attitude has changed also. When they were little, they would chuckle uncontrollably as they watched you eat, and at supper time, their little friends would flock over to watch Uncle Splatter suck up spaghetti at near-warp speed. You taught these young, eager learners that the faster the spaghetti enters the mouth, the farther the sauce flies—a basic law of physics that was proven over and over again at your dinner table. And let's not forget who taught the neighbourhood kids that the dinner table is no place to burp or belch, unless it is a medical emergency, such as a trapped air bubble.

Remember home-run derby, and all the fun that could be had with just a spoon and a plate full of peas? Remember the pride displayed by your children when Daddy took one deep, so deep that the dog was unable to find it. Good times, good times. It was Dad who taught the kids that life was full of hazards—to never let your guard down. A serious eye injury could be lurking across the table in the form of your father's out-of-control pork chop. This would serve them well, later on in life.

The glory days of family camaraderie around the supper table would soon end. As your children reached their teen years, they did not bring anyone around at mealtime. They would tell their little friends to stay away. "You can't come over because Dad has the flu. He's had it for seven years in a row now."

Perhaps my wife had finally gotten to them, or perhaps they had absorbed all the table lessons that they could handle. In any case, it seemed that everyone in the whole world had turned on you in respect to your eating habits; except your faithful dog. She would remain loyally at your feet during mealtime—on her back, with her mouth wide open.

However, there are still the guys at the local sports bar; friends who still appreciate a fine display of aggressive eating; a place where one could still hear the joyous calls of "incoming," during the chicken wing feeding frenzy. Call me old fashioned, but I feel that there is nothing like catching a well-aimed wing in the head, rescuing it before it hits the floor, and then eating it. Sharing food with your friends can be a very emotional moment. I can cry just thinking about it.

There have been some positive things to emerge from messy eating. My wife has invented a bib that is fashioned from one of those hairdresser capes. It closes tightly around the neck and has a wrap-around pocket on the bottom that captures any food shrapnel that falls straight down. I hope to market the supper tarp when it is perfected. It will be available in two colours, allowing the wearer to match the tarp with the type of gravy being served; chicken or beef. My dear wife does not feel the same way about me going public with the cover, but she has bought me two suits, yellow and brown. Incidentally, the dog growls when we get the supper tarp out.

My wonderful wife also invented the barbeque sauce pillow cover. She took one of my shirts to the local linen store and was able to match the stain to a sauce-coloured fabric. This was imperative because I am prone to burping in my sleep; and of course, with belching we get the accompanying drool. The pillow cover has an absorbent quality which is crucial—I no longer wake up with dried chicken wing barbeque sauce on the side of my face. I thank her for this piece of brilliance.

Also available, for those of us who lack culinary control, are the new hose-'em-off pants. We just discovered these recently, and they are truly a wonderful, wonderful product. It is impossible to stain these gems, even for the most aggressive eaters. How many times have you misplaced a chicken wing at the local sports bar, only to find it when you got up to go home? Your brother-in-law had not really stolen it; it was hiding on your lap for the last three hours. In the old days, you would have to walk out with an embarrassing stain right on your "groanal" area, and it might have been humiliating, but for the fact that most of the patrons were leaving in the same condition. This is nothing compared to the trouble waiting at home; your wife always found the pants, no matter how well you hid them.

There will be no more grief when you get home, if you are wearing these new hose-'em-off pants. Now, you can wash that stuff off with a well-aimed shot of beer before you leave the bar. Or, you can wait till you get home and garden-hose yourself before entering the house. No ugly stain—maybe a wet crotch, but the wife has come to accept this from time to time.

There is a bright side to being an aggressive eater. I have already mentioned that the dog just loves you to death at mealtimes. As I get older, my short term memory tends to fail me, but I don't have to remember what I had for supper last night. I need only to check my shirt pocket. Remember that mole on your back that you were told to watch? What a giant relief when it turns out to be nothing more than dried turkey gravy.

Buffet Tactics

Recent scientific studies have revealed that the eyelids of the Great White Shark automatically close when it feeds. This is a purely reflex action that has developed through millions of years of evolution, the sole purpose being to protect the eyes from the sharks' thrashing victims. This perhaps explains why the average married male sometimes gets lost on his way back from the buffet table.

A leading buffet scientist, tops in his field.

To begin this section of our eating disorder lesson, I once again fall back on raw scientific data, from not only a leading scientist, but from one who is obviously tops in his selected field. It says so right up there. I firmly believe that these little snippets of information give my amateur instructional manual a degree of professionalism, something that is sadly lacking in most other professional marital guides.

First, I would like to describe the origin and literal meaning of the word buffet. The earliest known recorded buffet was detected in the form of drawings on a cave wall. There, a cave woman can be seen laying out various cuts of mammoth, saber tooth tiger, a primitive form of chicken wing, and so on. The actual word for this feast was little more than a grunt that started with the letter B. From this, the French developed the word buffet, with the literal translation of, "a food-induced coma." This should give the Young Male a good background view of this wonderful, wonderful invention. I will now proceed with the lesson.

As *The Primer* (TP) developed, I would scour the announcement section of the newspaper in search of newlyweds with whom I could put my recently acquired skills and techniques to good use. Long before this, I would peruse the paper for a different reason. I would scout out buffets in the immediate area, looking for a certain type. Here is where the majority of young married males make their mistake.

The older, more experienced married male will not be baited by the theme buffets. These include the breakfast buffet, the spinach buffet, or the different-coloured-jello buffet. No, the more experience married male will accept nothing less than the Holy Grail of buffets, the All-You-Can-Eat Buffet, or, as it is known down at the local sports bar, "a little bit of heaven on a hell of a long table."

Total enjoyment of the buffet can only be achieved with total preparation, and as the title of the lesson indicates, there are certain buffet tactics that must be utilized. Luckily, I have done the leg work in this area, and by following my simple but effective lesson plan, the Young Male will be able to enjoy the event to the fullest. (No pun intended.)

Let us begin. You have done the scouting and have found a suitable buffet in your neighbourhood. You are wearing a lovely suit and are about to leave the house. Does anyone see anything wrong with this picture? This is the first mistake a Young Male will make; not taking the time to don the right clothes or, as we call it down at the local sports bar, buffet wear. Through trial and error, I have come up with the ultimate apparel for fine over-indulging, but not before I experienced a lot of heartache and grief.

Avoid pants with a belt. This will not work. Studies have shown that the expansion rate, required during a properly eaten buffet, is many times faster than the time it takes to loosen the belt a notch. As you fidget with your belt, you are already doing serious damage to vital organs that lie just below the skin at waist level. And don't even consider starting the buffet with your belt in its last notch, or as we say, "the end of the trail." There will be times during the buffet when sprinting will be required, and the humbling consequences of losing your pants on the way to the table far outweigh any advantage of pre-undoing.

Pants that button up are not only a serious mistake, but can be down-right dangerous when the buttons let go, and they will. Remember Young Males, there are powerful forces at work here and they must be respected. Particularly offensive are the multiple button-down pants so popular these days. All it takes is one button to weaken, then you have not one, but a series of projectiles flying across the room.

Fortunately, the offenders wearing these weapons are easy to spot. They have red faces and are not breathing very well. If you see someone who matches this description at an all-you-can-eat, let it be your duty to approach him and kindly ask him to undo his pants before some senseless tragedy occurs. A married male with any kind of a conscience will understand your request, and probably thank you. If he doesn't undo, seat your family as far away from him as geographically possible, and not directly facing him. Remember, there is a tremendous amount of latent energy entrapped inside a buffet eater's pants, and supper-table-safety is the key.

This leaves only one possible solution—buffet wear invented for people who know all about expansion and belly discomfort—pregnancy pants. I cursed those years that I suffered in vain when the answer was right there in my wife's drawers. Her now unused pregnancy apparel could be put to good use at the all-you-can-eat. These pants employ a special space-age elastic band that has the uncanny ability to expand over the long haul (nine months), or the short duration (thirty minutes). Unfortunately, I am taller than my wife by at least a foot, and while the stomach area seemed to fit fine, there was a gaping space between the hem of the pants and my shoes. One of the misfortunes of living in a small town is that the people at the local maternity store know that your wife is not, and never will be, six feet six inches tall. They refused to lengthen the pants. My wife failed to see the importance of this whole thing, so I was forced to rectify the situation myself.

I sewed a foot of new pants on the bottom of the old ones, matching up the colour fairly well. This task enabled me to use her power sewing machine. Although it took a little getting used to, I figured that if it plugs in and if it makes a bit of noise, then it must be a power tool. Unlike most power tools, it really can't hurt you unless it falls off the table onto your foot, and that only happened twice.

So there you have it, Young Males, proper buffet wear. Let's continue on to the buffet.

We are here in the parking lot and common sense tells us to park as close to the door as possible. I don't think I need to go into this in detail. If all goes according to plan, you will need assistance getting back to your car, and the further the wife has to carry you on her back, the grumpier she is going to be. This is common knowledge to most married males.

Once inside, we can get down to actual buffet tactics, and what is involved in making this a successful dining event. Peruse the buffet table, taking particular interest in how much there is of each dish. This will alert you as to which entree will go fastest, and should therefore be attacked first. Select your table, looking for one in the close proximity of the food. A distant table means more sprinting which brings aerobics into the equation, and we are not here for a workout—at least not in an exercising sense. If there is someone already seated in a prime location, there are subtle ways of dealing with this. I find that using a cane and standing at the occupied table for a brief period works fairly well. Also, limping around the table in pain will sometimes give them the hint. Your imagination is the only limiting factor here; there are endless possibilities.

We are now ready to get underway. Properly seated, properly attired in the buffet pants, and waiting for the word from the waiter. The word is given, and as you spring to your feet, you gaze over at the buffet table and discover a line stretching to what appears to be a mile long. It's time for some buffet tactics.

We try to create a diversion in another part of the restaurant. I have found that young kids are best for this; use your own, or pay someone else's youngster. The main thing is to get all those people interested in why that little child is crying in the far corner. Most people with a shred of moral value will go tearing over to see if they can help. That's your cue and you head for the now-deserted buffet table.

Another effective means of dealing with a crowd is getting in line, and suddenly announcing, "Please, let me through. I'm the local fowl inspector. I have some major concerns with the turkey; it's not supposed to be that colour, and I believe there's still some hair left under its wing. Everyone put down their forks."

Or, I may come dressed in bib overalls and straw hat. I focus on the ham, saying, "I raised that pig we're about to eat. It up and died on me all of a sudden. Maybe I should have been more careful in what I fed him. I hope they've cut out the diseased parts and then cooked it real good. Nope, I think I see a bad spot."

A last resort, regarding long buffet lines, is to simply bulldoze your way to the front. That's right; you go up and over their backs. Most patrons want to avoid confrontation, and unless you injure them seriously, they will just yell at you a bit and then forget about it—until you do it again later on.

The selection of an eating plate is crucial. Do not, under any circumstance, go with the allotted plates at the end of the buffet table. These are for rookies, and you will not get anywhere near the end of the spread before it is full. Glance over at the salad bar. There, you will see a large tray, full of cut up veggies. As discreetly as possible, dump the contents under the buffet table—all the while looking around for any nosy busybodies who are not minding their own business. If someone takes exception to your actions, inform them that you are the local vegetable inspector and luckily, you spotted some powdery mildew on the produce. I carry fake ID for just such an occasion.

You are all set with tray in hand and first in line. The actual eating of the buffet is pretty cut and dried. The main thing is that you have paid a certain amount of money for the all-you-can-eat, and you owe it to your family to get your money's worth. Use the same tray over and over again; waiters tend to get suspicious when their entire night is focused on gathering a multitude of dirty vegetable trays from one patron.

You want to eat your buffet fast for a couple of reasons. One, the good stuff, such as veal and ribs, tend to go very quickly, and you will want to score as much of these dishes as humanly possible. The other reason is purely scientific. I again refer to a leading buffet scientist, also tops in his field, who reports that studies have shown a direct correlation between the brain and feeling full. The trick is to devour a tremendous amount of food in the least amount of time, before the brain senses fullness. When it does sense the full condition, it alerts the other parts of the body involved in the buffet event and commands them to stop the eating process. Disregarding the message from the brain can lead to early warning signs. These may include a slight fullness in the stomach and some partial paralysis of the eating arm. It is best to gorge yourself quickly before these nuisance alarms go off.

However, eating fast does bring some real dangers, and one should be prepared. Both my children have been masters of the Heimlich maneuver since they were old enough to go stand in the corner and cry, and they have used this wonderful lifesaving method numerous times. I have developed a universal sign for "buffet down the wrong way," which will result in my children springing into action.

It is not a good idea to count on your wife when food goes down the wrong pipe. She is fine with doing the maneuver the first few times, but after a while, she has had enough. You will find yourself face down in your dinner tray, with your wife pounding away on the back of your head with her purse. Not only is this modified version of the Heimlich ineffective in clearing vast quantities of food from your windpipe, but do the patrons at the neighbouring tables really want to see this sort of thing? The for-better-or-worse promise has its limitations.

Another side effect of serious buffet eating is the oxygen-to-brain ratio that is severely affected when you are in full swing. We tend to slack off on our breathing, possibly because of the large volume of food traffic near our airways. A leading scientist, again tops in his field, has scientific proof that food rushing down the throat creates a Ventura effect that starves the air-pipe of oxygen. Air, that is supposed to go to the brain, ends up in your stomach where it must be burped up immediately—a slightly rude, but non-serious side effect. You do not have to observe a buffet master to know he is in the premises. You can hear him, again and again, clearing the trapped air from his stomach region.

When the air ends up in your stomach, your brain suffers. Buffet Brain Paralysis is the leading cause of premature buffet termination. Let me briefly describe what happens in the body, but I warn you, it is quite clinical and not easily understood by the layman. The food enters the stomach and is immediately processed by three major organs; the large and small esophagusses, the gizzard, and the liver and onions. Air that is not belched up enters the blood vessels and goes to various locations. That's all I know.

The Young Male must learn to identify the symptoms of Buffet Brain Paralysis. You find yourself going to the salad bar, gnawing on a carrot stick, or, heaven forbid, calling for the check prematurely. I know of one tragic instance where a man ate nothing but orange jello for an hour before someone noticed that he was in trouble. If this should happen to you, stop eating for a moment and clear your mouth of all food. Breathe deeply and put your head between your knees. (Studies have shown a greater concentration of oxygen-enriched air near the floor of most restaurants.) Be careful that you don't erroneously indicate that you are choking; this would be a bad time for your wife to activate her version of the Heimlich maneuver.

Because the physical symptoms of Buffet Brain Paralysis are not unlike those of heat stroke, we do not jump to any conclusions in the diagnosis. You may not have paralysis; you may have wedged your head between the heat lamp and the roast beef. As serious as this seems, you need only a quick trip to the hospital, and then you are back in the line up, bulldozing your way to the front again. And let me say this about our fine staff at the local emergency room. I do not believe that I have ever seen a more qualified group of dedicated people; true professionals who can treat one ear for third degree burns and pump beef gravy out of the other one—all the while, giggling about some joke.

In closing our segment on buffets, let me warn the Young Male that endurance at the table is best achieved gradually. The basic buffet tactics illustrated here can be learned and administered as your body progressively works its way to full acceptance of large quantities of food. As stated earlier, you owe it to your family to do your very best at the all-you-can-eat, but be wary of any warning signs that your body may give you. It is indeed a learning process.

The Young Male's Marriage Primer informs as well as teaches. This is never more prevalent than in describing the eating disorders of the average married male. We can take heart in the fact that leading archeology scientists have established, beyond a shadow of a doubt, that our disorder is indeed genetic—passed down from our cave ancestors, and we cannot do a darn thing about it.

I just might barbeque some mammoth steaks tonight, smear the grease all over my face, and watch all the neighbourhood women gather around me—not the big-boned ones with nice personalities, but the choice, prime females.

The Young Male's Marriage Primer
Lesson Thirteen

Getting into Shape for Your Wife
and for the Winter Olympics

Dr. Murray Dick

Dear Dr. Murray Dick,

I asked my wife the other day if I could still take her breath away, and if so, when was the last time. She replied that yes, I could, and the last time was when I fell on her at the legion dance on New Year's Eve. We've gone dancing a few times since, but I find the accompanying paramedics a bit stifling romantically. My wife recently took out a restraining order on me that is in effect only at dances. I'm not allowed within twenty-five feet of her. Slow dancing just doesn't seem the same anymore. I need your advice.

Preston (not my real name)

Dear Preston (not my real name),

I have read your letter over many times, but until I garner more information concerning your problem, I will not be able to make a complete diagnosis, closely followed by an amateur solution. For instance; are your wife's bones brittle? Perhaps she needs more calcium in her diet. Has she considered wearing goalie equipment at these functions? Can you still weigh yourself at home? The paramedics wouldn't be Margo and Fletcher by any chance? If so, I find them good company at socials and they are very discreet about blabbing that kind of stuff around. Your real name wouldn't be Clarence Crumbleford would it? If so, let me remind you that it is a cardinal sin to steal, and eat, a whole plate of chicken wings when the rightful owner is in the bathroom. It is you, isn't it Clarence? You owe me a plate of wings.

Let's get back to your problem, and allow me to speak professionally. The good news is that there is a stomach stapling procedure available. The bad news is that they are going to charge you by the staple. And don't forget about my chicken wings, Clarence.

Hope this helps,
Dr. Murray Dick

Once again, we start a lesson with an actual question submitted during one of my ever-popular seminars, Ask Dr. Murray Dick. These informative sessions are conducted regularly down at the local sports bar. The opening inquiry is indeed appropriate because this chapter deals with the physical condition of the average married male, and how to rectify this.

Although *The Primer's* curriculum was developed for Young Males, this particular lesson shows the foresight and vision of my great marriage manual. The key here is that you will not always look and function, as you do today. By carefully following the training habits and regiment outlined in this chapter, the Young Male will be able to maintain a high degree of bodily fitness, not unlike my own.

We were all virile and well-conditioned when we first got married. (That might be a lie.) Our wives worshipped us and were crazed with desire for our bodies. (Okay, that was one for sure.) The years can be unkind to the unwary married male and he can fall into the trap of not caring about his body and its growing size. All too soon, the only interest your body holds for your wife comes in the form of squeezing pimples, and for extracting back, ear, and nose hairs.

As the owner of a lucrative at-home woodworking business, I know how to drive my wife delirious with wanton desire in regards to my body. All I have to do is come into the house and announce, "Honey, will you dig out a sliver for me?"

Donning her safety glasses, she practically runs to me with a needle that could double as a tent peg. Her sliver removal gear also includes ear protection because she doesn't like to hear a grown man cry. I do admit that I may whimper a little bit, but what man wouldn't when your wife applies a tourniquet somewhere between the sliver and your heart.

When she is finished sewing me up (her record is fifty-five stitches), and she has vacuumed all the skin and blood from the floor, she sits down at the kitchen table and sighs. I believe that she would have a cigarette, if she was a smoker. *The Primer* refers to this activity as Middle Age Intimacy, and the degree of intimacy is directly proportional to the number of pimples on your back, or slivers in your hand.

Thus, it is imperative that no one, no matter how good of shape he is in, skip this tutorial; it will come back to haunt him in the future. He must do as I do. He must treat physical fitness, not as a one-time thing, but as a lifestyle.

Once again, I rely on my patented, revolutionary, Teaching by Example (TBE) technique, as I take the student back through my early years as a superstar athlete. The apprentice will also be amazed at how I keep my body in tiptop condition—even today, sporting a physique that men of all ages would be proud of.

I guess it was about grade four or five that the girls started to take notice of me, and boy, did they ever check me out—especially after lunch. It wasn't until later that I found out why. They had never seen one kid wear that much lunchbox food on his shirt.

Like most highly trained athletes, I was blessed with fast-twitch muscles, and they served me well on the school playground, where I was to become a legend.

I excelled at team sports and I remember tag and red rover as being two of my stronger activities—although I did start slowly in both of these events. If I recall, I was "it" for a whole year in tag, and none of the kids would "call me over" in red rover due to time constraints at recess. Eventually, I did blossom into a fierce competitor in both sports, and I was quite disappointed to learn that they did not give scholarships for either of these activities at the college level.

I graduated grade eight as captain of the red rover team and as assistant captain of the tag team. Entering high school, I found that these two team sports were not offered, and after trying in vane to organize an intramural league, I decided to retire. As with most athletes who hang them up, I tended to put on a little weight. The girls were still noticing me, and I dare say they were staring at me more than in my earlier athletic days. (The school offered hot lunches with lots of gravy.)

I filled my days with student activities instead of sports; becoming the primary voice in hot political school topics. It was I who rallied the students to press for a bigger deep fryer in the school kitchen. It was I who led the protest march for platters instead of plates in the cafeteria. When the Hostess Twinkies were discontinued in the vending machine, it was I who alerted the student body by running down the school halls yelling, "Save the Twinkies, Save the Twinkies!"

By the time I got married, my physique was quite substantial by most standards. Like the majority of young couples, my wife and I had pet names for each other. I would refer to her as "Princess Face," and she lovingly called me "Conan the Barbarian." (It was the cutest little thing.) A little while ago, feeling nostalgic, I called her Princess Face and she asked me where the heck that came from. I replied that it was her pet name from years ago, and it would not bother me in the least, if she addressed me in the same manner. She asked if I wanted to be called Princess Face and I said "No, use my pet name that you had given me."

She couldn't remember it, so I hinted that it was a famous movie figure of great size. She called me "Jabba the Hut" for a couple of days until the romantic aspect of the whole thing wore off.

Let us move on to the present, and I must say that my physical condition is much better than the average married male. It seems like never a day goes by that some young person asks, "Gee Dr. Murray Dick, you are a large burly man, but you carry that extra weight so well. How do you do it with your busy schedule?"

I always thank them for being so brutally honest. I go on to tell them about the training regiment that I employ, right in my workshop. I have quite a few different work stations from which I hustle back and forth, covering several feet in the course of a day. I never sit down— unless of course, I have a snack stashed at a particular station and even then, I'm only there for an hour on average.

Recently, I have noticed a change in the old body; I've had to shop in the large and chubby section of the Tools 'R Us Store for tool belts. I decided, then and there, that no matter how marvelous I looked, I was going to get into better shape. I was able to obtain a couple of free passes to the local fitness club, and after borrowing some running shoes and an old athletic supporter, I made my way down to the gym. To my astonishment, I found that it was located right next to the local sports bar. Dehydration would not be a problem; I could just slip next door every now and then for a cold one. And wonder of wonders, this workout place had showers. Never again would I have to drive home with chicken wing barbeque sauce all over my lap.

The first thing that I noticed upon entering the fitness centre was the amazing amount of exercise equipment. At least I think it was exercise equipment—I didn't recognize any of the apparatus. There were people running while going nowhere, people riding bikes while going nowhere, and people rowing boats going nowhere. However, there were TVs all over the place and finally, here was something that I was familiar with. I dragged one of the rowboat things over in front of a television, put it in recline position, and laid back to watch the hockey game.

A couple of the neighbourhood ladies strolled by and said, "Hi there, Jabba."

I told them that it was Conan, Conan the Barbarian, but they were too busy giggling to hear.

Suddenly a guy yelled at me, "Hey buddy, can you spot me?"

I cheerfully yelled back. "Well, yes I can. You're lying on a bench with a big pipe on your chest."

He looked at me kind of funny-like and told me to get over there. He was a large, beastly man, and he made me stand in front of his head while he pushed the pipe up and down. The plates on the ends were clinking away, and by the sound of his grunting and groaning, he seemed to be enjoying the whole episode. I was busy counting the number of plates on the pipe, when I spotted a fly landing on his stomach. Realizing that this was probably the reason I was there, I snuck around, and with a mighty swing I whacked the life out of that pesky insect. This seemed to surprise the fellow and the weight came crashing down on his chest. I believe that he would have attacked me had he not been pinned to the bench.

He started to make these little wispy sounds that occur when someone gets the wind knocked out of him. However, he was still able to reach up and wildly grasp for my throat. Between the little gaspy sounds, I think I detected a death threat, so I stepped back out of his reach.

I thought it was time to explore the far end of the gym, and I came upon a lady with a weighted pipe on her shoulders, squatting down and rising back up. This seemed like a great way to start. I loaded up my own pipe and hefted it onto my shoulders. Looking back, I now realize that I made two mistakes. The first error was putting different weights on either side, and the second was not securing them to the pipe.

I was about halfway down when I capsized to the left. The heaviest weight shot off the pipe and rolled over to the woman. Now, I do not believe for a minute that it was going that fast, but it caught her on the ankle while she was bending way down and she collapsed. For the second time in five minutes, I had pinned someone down with their own pipe.

I quickly exited to a different part of the gym with the lady in hot pursuit. I believe that she would have caught me, if she hadn't been crawling and clutching at her ankle. She also felt obligated to stop and help the large, beastly man, still pinned to the bench.

I came upon an apparatus called the pull-up bar, and I figured this might be as safe as anything else. It was while I was looking around for the instructional sheet that a woman approached me and mentioned that perhaps I should leave before I got hurt. I told her that I would stick to the safer equipment, but she revealed that the real danger was the clientele; at least two, or maybe more, wanted to beat the life out of me. She said that she was a personal trainer and I introduced myself, thinking she would recognize me as the author of the soon-to-be award-winning tutorial, *The Young Male's Marriage Primer*. I mentioned that with my leadership skills, perhaps I could be one of these trainers. She replied that none of the personal trainers found it necessary to carry a gun, and with that being said, she escorted me out.

The whole ordeal showed me how cruel some people can be to a newcomer. Instead of being embraced and welcomed, now I'm being stalked by a large, beastly man, and a woman with a bad ankle. I plan to return to the gym soon, but I will be wearing the new Kung Fu outfit my wife made for me, complete with lavender belt. (She said black wasn't in this year). This, along with some well-practiced, vigorous chopping motions, accompanied by blood-curdling screams, should get me the respect I deserve. In the words of my idol, Conan the Barbarian, "I'll be back!"

You know, Young Males, it is amazing how one trip to the gym can improve your body, both physically and mentally. I felt invigorated. I felt newborn. I was ready to embrace one of my numerous lifelong dreams; I was going to train, and participate, in the next Olympics Games.

Because of my past success in team sports at elementary school, I decided that this would be my direction in selecting an event. I chose my brother-in-law Wally as a teammate, and I mentioned to him that he should make at least one trip to the fitness centre to become invigorated and newborn. He replied that this was one of the town's many establishments where he had been banned.

We chose my house to sit down and discuss which sport we were likely to excel. Overhearing us, my wife suggested that we should try synchronized diving. She recalled our last vacation at the cottage, where Wally and I both fell off the dock at exactly the same time. Never had she heard such applause from the other cottagers, even hearing remarks on how graceful we were. They talked about it for weeks. My wife also commented that hypothermia shouldn't be a problem, not when we sported the blubber that a whale would envy. She also said that we should work on our entry; the judges may deduct marks if half of the pool water is removed by the splash. In addition, she said that most synchronized divers do not scream for help on their way into the water. Wally would have to work on that. Other than these trivial items, she thought we stood a great chance of making the Canadian team. Isn't it marvelous when you have a wife who takes a proactive role in your endeavours?

This diving thing made good sense to Wally and me, but after researching the sport, we found that the pool used at the Olympics is deep—well over the diver's head. As you probably know by now, Wally is quite the aquatic safety advocate—and for good reason. He can't swim. He often cites alarming statistics about non-swimmers diving into unknown waters without first checking the depth, and then finding themselves in peril when trying to get back to dry land. Wally always checks the water level first, and if it is over his waist, he will not dive in. Once again, my brother-in-law "walks-the-walk" when it comes to aquatic safety.

It was Wally's idea to compete in the two-man bobsled competition. He explained that the majority of activities making up the Winter

Olympic events were common-place. Most people in our little town were already skiing and ice-skating. While no one had the talent necessary to gain Olympic status, it was a good bet that all of these folks were a sight better at these sports than the two of us.

Bobsledding is different. Not one person in our town has a bobsled. By merely owning a bobsled, we would immediately become the best bobsledders for miles and miles around. It made excellent sense to me and we proceeded with our lifelong dream of the past two weeks, of owning and driving a two-man bobsled.

You talk about good luck; I was able to find a sled on an internet auction, and my bid of ten dollars was not only the lone offer, but the winning one as well. I pride myself on my ability to haggle incredible deals, and sometimes I wonder why other people do not take advantage of steals, such as my bobsled purchase.

After paying the three thousand dollar shipping fee, I helped unload the sled from the delivery truck. I believe that my wife was thinking about neighbourhood jealousy when she told the men to drag it into the backyard—way back behind the garden.

I asked the delivery driver where the nearest bobsled run was. He pointed west and said, "Calgary, Alberta. Give us another three grand, and we'll drive both you and the sled there."

Wally's prognosis was dead-on. We were now the best sledders in our little town, or even all of Ontario for that matter. We would, however, have to train in the backyard.

The bobsled is an event fraught with excitement, danger, and uniforms that make women delirious with desire. They are skintight and formfitting to cut down on wind-resistance, and we all know that women really like this kind of stuff. Wally and I went down to the local men's clothing store, where I asked the lady if she could fit my friend and me in bobsled suits. She replied that she was sorry, but the last two had just been purchased by a couple of big, fat penguins. She went on to say that this was unfortunate; the sled uniforms would have fit us perfectly. Wally and I quietly left the store before her tone became sarcastic.

As luck would have it, we spotted a pair of old skin-diving wet-suits in the army surplus store, and they seemed to resemble official bobsled uniforms. We purchased these gems and headed home to the basement. It was time to suit up for our first training run. It soon became evident that these outfits either belonged to children, or to a very short race of people who enjoyed skin diving. People pay good money for a workout similar to the one that Wally and I obtained by merely wedging into our new uniforms.

We were finally dressed, and as I looked at my training partner, with his hockey helmet on and his face beet-red from exertion, the Olympic spirit hit me. A few short moments ago, we were merely mortal men, but now, we were competitors—ready to give our all, in the name of sportsmanship, strength, and courage. As I called for my wife to help us up the stairs, I have never been so proud to be a man.

Wally and I stood in front of her in the living room, and I could sense the positive impression we were exhibiting. I expected an outpouring of craving and desire, and although my wife probably felt these things deep inside, she was able to control her wanton emotions in front of Wally. She did say that we might want to move some bulges around to different places, if our intent was to impress bobsled chicks. She also said that she did not remember Jabba the Hut wearing anything like that in the movie. Our conversation was cut short when she thought she heard some fabric letting go. She ran into the bathroom, locking the door. I know my wife, and I believe that she was both proud and excited in her own little way.

We waddled to the backyard for our first practice. Unfortunately, our yard is level and because the sled was heavy, we had to alter our training. It is very hard to believe that two men can master the bobsled without it ever moving an inch, but Wally and I did. As we settled into the sled, I noticed two things. One, it was an extremely tight fit, and perhaps I should have bid on a four-man bobsled. Two, I realized that we either did not have any brakes, or I didn't know where they were. A lot of people fail to realize the importance of brakes on a bobsled. There are certain times when engaging the braking system is critical—such as when your run is finished and you want to exit the sled safely. For Wally and I, this was crucial. According to the little sticker inside, our combined weight exceeded the manufacturer's specifications for this particular sled—actually exceeding it by about two hundred pounds. There was no doubt that Wally and I would fly down the run – gravity, acting on our tremendous mass, would see to that. If, by chance, we ever made it to the closest bobsled site, our problem would be stopping before we flew into downtown Calgary.

It was Wally who came up with the idea of cutting holes in the bottom of the sled and using our feet to stop. He had seen this very same thing done on a cartoon show. Wally, an out-of-work master plumber who, as you know, likes to dabble in psychiatry, is a true thinker. We all watch cartoons and a few of us even laugh at the appropriate times, but who among us has the vision and the foresight to put the ideas, garnered from these shows, to practical use? I am proud to be related to this man through marriage, and I could not have asked for a better bobsled partner. If we ever got our sled moving, I was quite confident that we would be able to stop it safely.

We also learned that it wasn't just how good we looked that impressed our women, but also the dangers that all bobsledders encounter. The changes in environmental conditions are cruel; snow, freezing rain, sleet, nighttime darkness, kids throwing frozen vegetables at us, and distracting neighbourhood women yelling, "Go Jabba, go."

It goes without saying that helmets are mandatory; birds just love taking dead aim at a stationary target. It also seemed that our dog Bailey was trying to bite us, when all she wanted to do was to crawl inside to warm up. Once there, she licked our visors until we were running blind as a result of excess dog saliva.

The start in bobsledding may be exciting to watch, but it is extremely hazardous. Because the sled was sitting on flat ground, making it impossible to move, we had to alter our starting procedure. We would run on the spot with reckless abandon, screaming like banshees. Wally, ever the enthusiast, chipped a tooth when he kneed himself in the jaw. (He soon learned to take them out before practice.) He became so adept at running and jumping into the sled, that he only entered it face-first half the time. I actually preferred this style of entrance, as opposed to feet-first, where I was continually kicked in the head. You can see why we bobsled drivers wear helmets.

I like to think that we became excellent bobsledders, learning to lean and crouch when birds approached and other things too technical to delve into here. Unfortunately, the true danger of this sport was to become all too evident. One day, we were going into the last curve on a pretend practice when Wally's suit let go. My first indication was a slight creaking noise from behind me as the fabric started to give way. This was soon followed by a loud ripping sound, and a low, somewhat happy moan escaping from Wally. I then got the sensation that somebody was spraying expanding insulating foam inside the sled, causing my face to become jammed against the windshield. Also, Bailey the dog got squirted out and landed over the fence.

The run ended when we realized that we were trapped in the bobsled. Yelling for help did no good—perhaps because the neighbours thought we were just practicing our start again by screaming like banshees. Luckily, Wally always rides with a cell phone and after the fire truck arrived, the neighbours finally realized that something was terribly wrong.

The firemen were very good, talking to us in a calming voice when they weren't doubled over in laughter. Actually, Wally said he felt great—the best he'd been in days. If anyone ever has the chance to watch these men use the Jaws of Life up close, you will be impressed. They opened up that sled like a can of beans and had us out in less than three or four hours. The pictures they took will probably end up in one of those firemen calendars. A loud cheer from the onlookers greeted our escape, and even my wife, hiding in the house to allow me my moment of glory, was undoubtedly excited.

In conclusion, let me remind the Young Male, that while taking up a dangerous sport like bobsledding can be rewarding, even resulting in newspaper fame, it should only be tackled by highly trained athletes, such as Wally and I. Only a wonderful role model, such as me, would issue warnings to those of you who are merely amateurs.

Wally and I have tasted the thrill of living on the edge and looking good in our formfitting bobsledding uniforms. The sled still sits in the backyard, and every now and then, I go back there just to sit and think of our Olympic experience. It is a beautiful spot in our garden that I treasure dearly. Someone painted the name "Hut-mobile" on the front and the birds have been using it quite frequently, turning it a lovely ivory colour.

Words are ineffective in describing our thrill of victory and our agony of defeat. We were victorious in every practice run, although there was some agony involved when Wally's bobsled suit let go. Like most Olympic athletes, it is the camaraderie and the spirit of the games that are most important to us. However, we are not so humble as to admit that winning a gold medal for our country is equally satisfying. I constructed a podium out of special plywood, imported from all the way down the road at Gus's Lumber and Marriage Manual Store. When Wally and I stood on that platform to receive our medals, our emotions were running high.

We were wearing special bobsled warm-up suits that my wife had made, and although we felt they covered up our sleek, formfitting uniforms, my wife informed us that she could still see the bulges. She guaranteed us that we would continue to attract any sled chicks who might be hanging out in the backyard.

In a clear, loud voice, Wally and I sang the parts of the Canadian National Anthem that we knew off-by-heart, and mumbled our way through the rest of the song. As we came to the end, the emotion of the ceremony was too much for us, and we both finished in a jumble of singing, weeping, and mumbling. It is a moment that all Olympic athletes should be aware of, and prepared for, when the time comes. Wally and I practice the medal ceremony every week.

I do not expect the Young Male to take physical fitness to the extent that I have. He should set his goals a little lower when first starting out. Remember, Wally and I are highly trained athletes, and we watched quite a bit of bobsledding on the big screen down at the local sports bar before attempting any perilous pretend runs.

Please keep this in mind. Your young wife could develop the desire and craving that our spouses possess, if only you take care of yourself. Remember, staying in shape is not only a life-long commitment—but also a lifestyle.

The Young Male's Marriage Primer
Lesson Fourteen
Role Models

Dr. Murray Dick

As stated earlier in *The Primer*, married life is strewn with pitfalls, confusion, and terror. It is very hard for the Young Male to travel this road alone and achieve the lofty marital levels that I have attained in my own highly successful marriage. Today's lesson deals with role models; people who play an important part in everyone's life. This is especially true for the young married male. He needs someone to look up to, someone who has been there, done that, and someone who is more than willing to pass along the information needed—not only to survive, but to excel.

In this lesson, I will attempt to cover a wide variety of role models, or as I like to call them, local heroes. This selection will allow the student to choose one that either fits his lifestyle, or he would like to emulate. We will start off with a well-known local hero, yours truly.

I realize that I state the obvious when I consider myself a role model. I am not afraid to admit my mistakes, and that's not counting the ones coming up in the future. However, I learn from these errors and I turn them into teachable moments for my students. I can then reach out to the Young Male, define his problem, and use the tools necessary to solve the dilemma. The following Primer Case Study (PCS) illustrates this point.

We hear of one specific problem in the news every single day. A big sports star is caught taking stimulants of some kind to enhance his or her performance. The monetary rewards seem to overshadow the moral ethics of fair play. I have travelled this route before, and I know the dangers all too well. My experience now allows me to guide my young followers down the right path.

I took a case of beer fishing once. It did not enhance my ability to catch fish, but it did enhance my ability to fall off the dock. A couple of kids scooped me up in a landing net and they said that it was their biggest catch of the summer. They were impressed enough to spread the news around our small town, and soon, a picture of me in the net showed up on the local sports bar wall. Someone even drew fins on me. Now, all of my motivational speeches endorse taking iced tea on fishing trips. Performance enhancing stimulants, such as beer, can tarnish even the best of reputations—as I have found out.

Another local sports bar hero is Farley Drellhurst. Farley left school at an early age to pursue a career in agriculture and now runs a manure spreading operation in, and around town. He has a very large tractor and spreader, but the man has an uncanny ability of maneuvering in tight areas, such as backyards. If you have a garden that needs some fresh stuff, old Farley's your man; but you may want to close your house windows and garage doors. He has been known to "side" a few homes when he gets excited, or if he feels like spreading in high gear. Farley is now looking into franchising his operation, calling it "Blowing in the Wind."

You can find Farley in his own corner of the local sports bar, always willing to talk manure. If you do happen to see him, why not buy him a beer and take it over to him; the waitresses will be much obliged. Farley has one marital standard that he swears by—never take your work home with you.

My brother-in-law Wally is a wonderful role model. Wally, an out-of-work master plumber who, as you know, likes to dabble in psychiatry, recently renewed my faith in the human spirit. Stories abound of the hidden strength of human beings and their almost super-human ability to perform in times of great duress. For example, we have all heard the tale of the distraught mother who is able to summon the strength needed to lift a car when her child is in peril. Frankly, I've always been skeptical of this kind of heroics until that fateful night, down at the local sports bar, when one of Wally's chicken wings rolled under the juke box.

We have an uncanny ability of remembering exactly where we were when an astounding event occurs. When Wally lifted the juke box with one hand to retrieve his chicken wing down at the local sports bar, I will always remember where I was—I was down at the local sports bar. I thank Wally for renewing my faith in the human spirit.

Bert Toony deserves the ranking of genuine hero. Bert has been our school crossing guard down at the local intersection for the past thirty years, and although he has run afoul of the law recently, his reputation down at the local sports bar has never been questioned. Ever the entrepreneur, Bert noticed that our little town did not have a Squeegee Kid at our only intersection. Seeing how he was stopping vehicles for the kids, what was the harm in cleaning a few windshields for some pocket change?

Another plus for Bert is that he is fairly tall, and we get a goodly number of combines going through town. Bert has the height to deal with even the biggest machines, and on a good day, he can make anywhere from two to four bushels—and that's all take-home.

However, success soon turned sour for Bert. Because his regular working shift coincided with the children's schedule as they journeyed to and from school, he only worked a few hours in both the morning and afternoon. Greed can change a human being and Bert was no exception. He decided to extend his working day, stopping vehicles and cleaning their windshields, for a full eight hours. People began to realize that they were being stopped for no apparent reason. Some complained to town council, some sped up when they saw him approach, and some chased him over the lawns with their cars.

A reprimand was forthcoming, and during the investigation, it came to light that Bert was also taking the crossing guard equipment home for his personal use. It seems that he had been one of the few people listening to my motivational speech down at the bar last year. It was entitled, "A Woman Loves a Man in Uniform."

When questioned about this allegation, Bert replied. "It's true, a woman does prefer a man in uniform and don't let anyone tell you that a big man doesn't look good in florescent yellow, with a large X on his back."

I was going to ask him about the traffic cone and stop sign, but after careful consideration, I felt that some things should remain unsaid.

"Hawkeye" Bob Feener is another role model that the Young Male can look up to. We always knew that he had a keen interest in wildlife, and it was not uncommon for him to watch the National Geographic TV show. He called one afternoon and informed me that he had come upon an injured bird of prey, probably an eagle of some kind, and he was nursing it back to good health.

Bob went on to say that finding the injured raptor had inspired him, and he actually felt a calling. He was setting up a wildlife refuge where people could bring in wounded birds of all kinds, and for a nominal fee, Hawkeye Bob would use all of his skills to bring the birds back to life. He also wondered if I had one of those falcon gloves that he could use when the eagle regained consciousness. I told him no, I didn't have one, but I would ask around.

I next saw Bob down at the local sports bar and he was proudly showing off his injured bird of prey. He hadn't found a falconers glove, but he was wearing an old used golf glove, and the injured bird was duct taped to it. Someone pointed out to him that it wasn't really an eagle of some kind—it was a crow. It seems that the crow had gotten into some fermented corn down at the ethanol plant, and ironically, it had flown into the side of a beer truck parked in front of the local sports bar. It was also noted that the crow's head was limp, and hanging at an angle that strongly suggested it wasn't going to regain consciousness any time in the near future. Bob, ever the wildlife enthusiast and an optimist at heart, replied that he would work with the bird. When it did come to, he would tend to its wounds, and eventually nourish it with the dead mouse that he carried around in his pocket.

Another wonderful hero with a great story is Thomas Cringe, another friend and patron of the local sports bar. Most students will remember his anti-snore devices from an earlier lesson. They were truly wonderful inventions that didn't work. If the Young Male is looking for a man who shows ingenuity and free thinking, Tom is your man. At the ripe old age of eighty-eight, he decided to become an entrepreneur and open up a Bed and Breakfast. While this has been done numerous times, be advised that Thomas lives in a trailer park. Due to frequent violations in the past, he has been asked to leave many other parks, and his trailer is easily recognized as the only one with the wheels still on it. Although handy for quick get-aways during the night, many guests have awakened in the morning complaining of having no feeling in their legs, and a pulsing, thumping sensation in their heads. It seems that one tire has a slow leak, and by dawn, the severe list of the trailer has caused the travellers' blood to pool in their heads.

Another problem with the Bed and Breakfast is Thomas' temper. It is not uncommon for him to wake up in a foul mood, after a long night at the local sports bar, and pound on the weary sleepers' door yelling, "Get up, get out, there's no breakfast today!"

Our local Chamber of Commerce got so many complaints that Thomas was forced to change his sign to "Cringe's Bed and Possibly Breakfast." This has hurt his business, but on the brighter side, Thomas says that with fewer lodgers, he doesn't have to pump up the tire as often.

As stated earlier, Thomas is also our resident inventor, and like most free-thinkers, he recognized a need and he is currently capitalizing on it. This need deals with people his age. Through trial and error, Thomas found that teeth whitening strips work remarkably well on old yellow toenails. He just buys the strips from the local pharmacy, puts masking tape over the entire box, and with a magic marker writes, "Tom's Toenail Tinters." He also includes instructions, warranties and medical alert information.

For the moment, he sells these strips from his front porch, but look for this product in fine pharmacy stores everywhere in the near future. It really does work and I hope that the Young Males will stop by the trailer park and have a peek at Tom's toes. It will not cure the fungus, but you have to get your face right down there, within inches, to see any toe disease. He leaves one big toe "as is" to show the remarkable change. To view old Tom's toes from up close, and to witness the whitening and brightening, will surely take your breath away.

He also sells a wide variety of clippers ranging from small delicate ones for the young and fragile toenails—found mostly on teenagers; to bolt cutters for the old, gnarly toenails—found mostly on old people of the same description. Thomas' attitude on toenail fungus matches The Primer Philosophy perfectly. Why fix a problem, whether it be marital or toenail fungus, when you can gloss it over?

I began this lesson with myself as one of the many role models available, and I would like to end on the same note. As I get older, I find myself becoming more giving and caring. Recently, I asked my wife if she noticed this also. She replied, "Oh yeah, Doc', you're a real giving caregiver, that's for sure."

With this new caring attitude, I find myself more concerned about young people and their struggles to gain acceptance in a new environment. We see it everyday, someone joins a local service club or another fine established organization, and they do not fit in. No one pays them any attention, and they fade further and further into the background.

Not long ago, a fine young gentleman joined our local sports bar and I watched this lad on his first night there. It was a total disaster. However, it inspired me to take the next step in furthering my own impressive resume—to become a coach.

It seems that there are coaches for everything these days; personal coaches for sports, career coaches, personality coaches, life coaches, self-help coaches, and the list goes on. I could have chosen any of these and excelled, but I opted for a branch of coaching that is unusual. After watching the young man's demoralization, my choice was clear. The following story led me to my decision.

If the patrons of any local sports bar have anything in common, it is their willingness to tell stories. The more familiar the patrons are with each other, the more accepted their stories. The content of such tales becomes unimportant. A newcomer is not allowed this privilege, and the rookie in the local sports bar had better get a good start if he wants to be accepted by his peers. This is where the young man failed miserably. He attempted to tell a story on his first night, and it went like this:

I was out for a jog the other morning, actually on my way to yoga class, when I was approached by a lady walking her white, fluffy dog. I believe it was a poodle. It started to bark in a high-pitched, little yapping sound. While I was passing, it nipped me on the ankle. I swear that the lady gave it some slack for the sole purpose of allowing this vicious attack. Why can't pet owners be more responsible and control their leashed animals?

The comments of the locals following this story were predictable—
there were none. Not one soul was paying attention by the time the
young man had ended his dialogue. I sadly watched him sink back into
his chair in silence, and he remained that way for the rest of the evening.
I decided, then and there, that never again would I let a senseless
tragedy like this unfold. I would dedicate the entire following week to
the development of new techniques to help this fine young man and
others like him. I would take time off from my career as an amateur
marriage doctor, and also set aside any work in my lucrative, at-home
woodworking business. I was about to become an Exaggeration Coach.

For some reason, I have a natural gift in this field. In no time, I
was able to give this particular young patient his first lesson. We went
over his original story in detail, breaking it down to determine how it
failed. First, he lost half the local sports bar crowd when he mentioned
jogging. Just the thought of exercise turns these guys off, and you do
not attain the girth of these guys by doing anything close to hurrying.

He lost half of the remaining listeners (that might be a third
although I'm not sure) when he said that he was on his way to yoga
class. This may come as a shock, but guys who frequent local sports
bars do not go to yoga class, unless you count those who go peeking in
the windows to check out the flexibility.

The remaining three quarters of the men gave up when the lad
mentioned the white, fluffy dog. Now, a lot of the good stories down
there involve sympathy and heroics. You are not going to get much
empathy when your nemesis reminds them of a Smurf, especially if the
Smurf actually "takes you out." And let's just say that you did overcome
the white, fluffy dog. How heroic can strangling a Smurf be?

I coached the patient on these, plus other problem areas of his story.
In the short period of one week, he was prepared to try his narrative
once again at the local sports bar. Parts of his original account were
kept, such as the white, fluffy segment—although altered somewhat.
His new tale would be heavy on heroism and was intended to give the
listeners a wish-I-was-there kind of feeling. I believe that he captured
the intent rather well. The young lad's story went like this:

The other day, I was returning some Rambo tapes to the local video store on my Harley. Naturally, I was wearing no helmet, just feeling the wind rustling through my hair. I was shoeless also, again feeling the same breeze rustling through my toes. I was just debating about stopping off and donating some bone marrow for the third time that day down at the local bone marrow clinic, when I spotted quite a commotion on the sidewalk.

I sensed a medical emergency; I have an uncanny awareness of these things. I put my Harley into a power slide to stop quicker, got up off of the ground, and approached the gathering crowd. I yelled out, 'Let me through, I watch ER on a big-screen TV. Clear a path.'

In the brief flash of a second, I assessed the situation. A woman with the biggest belly that I have ever seen was lying and screaming on the sidewalk. I knelt down and asked her if she had fallen and couldn't get up. She replied no, she was about to give birth right there. I thought, 'holy crap! It would have been easier to try and lift her,' but I immediately took complete control of the situation.

I addressed a lad who looked like a strong runner, 'You, run down to the local hospital. In the front lobby, you'll find a pay phone. Call that 911 number! I don't remember what it is, but I think it starts with a nine. Someone lend him a quarter or a calling card.'

I turned my attention to the lady with the big belly. I told her to remain calm—I had watched this very same thing on Wild Kingdom and a warthog isn't a whole lot different than a human. I asked her to time her 'contraptions.' She didn't understand; she probably wasn't as well-versed as I in clinical terms regarding childbirth.

I would need 'birthing' equipment. I spotted a rather attractive young lady in the crowd and I said to her, 'We're going to need some sterile bath towels. If you don't have any in your purse, I'm afraid I'm going to have to commandeer your blouse. Don't worry about the buttons; time is our enemy. Just rip it off. There you go.'

My attention was now divided between the pregnant woman and the lady with no shirt on. 'Yes, she was quite attractive, maybe mid-twenties. No, she had no wedding ring on. I think it was the 'cross-your-heart' model; there wasn't much of it, I'll tell you. I've seen a couple of those up close in a catalogue.'

I was about to tell the shirt-less girl that I would soon be in need of a lacy, button-at-the-front tourniquet for the delivery, when I spotted something marauding through the crowd. It was fluffy and white. It was a three-ton polar bear down from Churchill, Manitoba. Did I say three? I meant four-ton and it was coming straight for me. I recognized it immediately. It was a garbage dump bear and we had crossed paths up in Churchill at the town dump. We had a big fight over some food and it appeared that this five-ton polar bear was bearing a grudge. And to make matters worse, it was unleashed.

You know, fellas, the whole time that I was administering first aid; I could feel the gaze of the lady without the blouse burning a hole in my back. Oh yeah, she liked me; liked me big time. I've never felt so violated or abused, although I've been close.

Now things got interesting. As I continued to administer medical attention, the bear reached me and bit me right on the butt. It took all of my training as an amateur paramedic to concentrate on the task at hand. Just before the delivery, I remember looking back, and yes, the bear was still there. Luckily, I have a high tolerance of pain. You know, men, I could have subdued that bear at anytime using mixed martial arts—I am well-versed in all of the disciplines. My entire body is a loaded weapon.

Well, to make a long story short, the delivery went as planned and I was able to find the leash, secure the polar bear, and return it to its rightful owner. The pregnant lady was so grateful that she named the newborn after me. My thoughts and prayers are with her new daughter, 'Barney Cassandra Norkfest.' I know she'll never forget me.

The shirtless woman became just another of my 'passing in the night' ladies. She's probably still thinking about me in a violating, abusing train of thought. A man can only dream.

And finally, why can't pet owners be more responsible and control their leashed animals?

The effect this story had on the patrons of the local sports bar was indeed stunning. When Barney finished, there was total silence; the patrons were enthralled. When everyone realized that the tale was over, cheers broke out. There were cries of, "Encore, encore," and the lad was forced to recount the episode—not the whole story, just the part about the lady with no shirt on. There was one awkward moment when someone demanded to see the bite marks, but he was shouted down. Most married males do not want this kind of information filtering back to their wives.

When I think back to all the good work that I have done for mankind, I believe that this could be my finest hour. Watching that young lad talk his way into the hearts of the patrons of the local sports bar gave me a truly wonderful feeling.

My hat goes off to Thomas, Hawkeye Bob, Wally, and all the other heroes down at the local sports bar. The danger in compiling such a list is that there is a chance that some deserving people are left off. Let me go on record in stating that every one of my friends down there possesses good qualities—qualities that would make them wonderful role models for the Young Male. We just have to look for the good in people, and these local heroes are full of it.

The Young Male's Marriage Primer
Lesson Fifteen
The Future of The Primer

Dr. Murray Dick

We have come to the end of *The Young Male's Marriage Primer*, a work dedicated to the betterment, of not only new bridegrooms, but of married males of all ages. There is great excitement in the world of amateur marriage doctoring, and I would like to conclude our lessons with a brief summary of recent happenings and also future updates pertaining to *The Primer*.

First of all, *The Primer* has sold out. Actually, all the copies were given away down at Gus Walmsly's place. If you recall, Gus is the proprietor of Gus's Lumber and Marriage Manual Store. My instructional tutorial wasn't moving too well (we did not sell any), and Gus said that he needed the space for roofing nails. He decided to give a free *Primer* to anyone who purchased a single sheet of plywood. Apparently, every housewife in town needed one sheet of plywood last week, and now every last copy of my work is gone. It seems that a lot of men in town will be getting special Christmas presents; something made out of wood, plus their very own *Primer*. I will have to go back to my publisher Stan Frenway, retired truant officer and current owner of Stan's Marriage Manual Publishing. Hopefully, he will allow me the use of his garage and also rent the printer and stapler for me. I plan on making twelve copies this time so we do not run out quite as fast.

Another area that has caught me completely by surprise is the celebrity status that I currently enjoy. Yes, the patrons down at the local sports bar think highly of *The Primer* and like most famous people, I have access to the seats closest to the TV. I have also noticed that during the food fights, the guys are less likely to aim their chicken wings at me. While this has been quite expected, it is the change in the women's attitude that has caused me some delightful moments.

I was in our drug store the other day, and the lady pharmacist announced over the loud speakers, "Dr. Murray Dick, your male enhancement prescription is ready at the counter."

Well, it's not everyday that one hears his name blared over a public address system, and as I proudly walked down the aisles, one local housewife called out to me, "Way to go there, Jabba."

Another woman yelled over, "Hey Dick, how's the 'Hut-mobile' doing these days?"

I must have been quite the sight, blushing with pride, as I approached the dispensary. I reluctantly informed the druggist that, although I deeply appreciated the special VIP treatment, I never ordered any such medication. She smiled at me, turned to her microphone, and once again spoke loudly and clearly over the speakers, "And it's the industrial strength stuff that you so obviously need, Dr. Dick."

Although it will take awhile, I believe that I could get used to this celebrity status thing. Did I mention that I was blushing with pride?

The Young Males Marriage Primer is, of course, a revolutionary marital manual, but it must always keep abreast of the ever-changing times. To carry on its remarkable success, *The Primer* cannot remain static. It was recently brought to my attention that young people have changed their tastes in music, and you can imagine my surprise when it was pointed out that they no longer listen to disco. Personally, I have always loved disco, and I hope that it never dies. I play little else on my phonograph.

One new form of music is called hippity-hop, and although I haven't a clue as to what it sounds like, the name itself conjures up some kind of rabbit-thing. It is nice to know that our youth are embracing a clean, physically active form of entertainment—hopping around like little bunnies.

Another popular variety of music to surface lately is entitled rap music. This is anything but traditional; the words of the song are spoken, while the music remains in the background. I had been toying with the idea of a marriage instruction music tape for quite some time, and after researching this rap thing, I was ready to "put down some tracks," as we say in the recording business.

Once again, I called upon my publisher Stan Frenway, owner of Stan's Marriage Manual Publishing, and he immediately came on board, donating the use of his eight-track recorder. Then, in an unprecedented display of conviction and confidence, Stan went out and borrowed a microphone.

I soon discovered that the most popular rap music being played today is called gangster rap. With this in mind, I invited our local felon, Bert Tooney, to do the rapping. Bert, if you recall, is the local school crossing guard who ran afoul of the law by taking his uniform and equipment home—for his personal use. Bert said that he would be glad to help and wondered if these rappers wore a special uniform. His wife had grown accustomed to the crossing guard florescent X emblem, and perhaps a new outfit would spice up his marriage. I told him that I would look into it, although I really didn't want to.

Another well known trait of rappers is how they wear their pants. They ride very low on their torsos and as everyone knows, no one wears trousers any lower than an out-of-work master plumber. Wally was invited to be the DJ, and as far as duplicating the low-hung pants, he did not disappoint us.

We were all set. "Grand Master Plumber Daddy" Wally spun a record this way and that on an old phonograph player while he made continuous burping noises with his mouth. This set a good rhythm for Bert, who did wonderfully well with reciting the words to the first, "Young Male's Marriage Primer Rapping 8-Track Instructional Tape." Check it out dude, it is especially groovy:

Yo Mama, gotta' tell ya and I give ya no jive
Gotta' make the man happy just to keep the love alive.
Get yo booty movin' and don't ya be no fool,
Do the right thing mama, buy the power tool.
Shuffle to the left, boogie to the right,
Stand up, sit down, fight, fight, fight.
Yo body's looking mighty fine, ain't no joke,
Get on down to Tools 'R Us, our table saw is broke.

It goes on and on, but I think the Young Male gets the idea of just how inspirational and topical this recording really is. We were able to obtain three copies before Stan's 8-track recorder succumbed to mechanical failure. However, we are hoping that in the future, a big recording company will sign us to a large contract.

Unfortunately, there is a sad note to all of this. Bert was enthralled with the DJ's pants, and after much begging and pleading, Wally allowed him to wear them home. He didn't get far before they released, and Bert tripped over himself. He is currently in a full-body cast. How this new uniform is affecting his married life is anyone's guess. With Bert, some things are best left unasked.

There has been a lot of talk lately about publishing *The Primer* in foreign languages. Actually, it has just been Wally and I talking, but we have been talking about it a lot. One night, down at the local sports bar, we met a man from Sweden that I have since learned is a small island country near Ethiopia. His name was Sven, but most of the guys had trouble in the pronunciation and it ended up sounding like Seven.

When asked if calling him this would bother him, he quipped, "Oh you can call me Sven, or you can call me Seven, just don't call me late for odenheyman."

This brought on hysterical bouts of laughter from all of us, although no one had the slightest idea why.

It turned out that Seven came from a very distinguished family. As you know, Sweden is a cold, barren country. Winter lasts all year round and because of these conditions, all children are forced to take a two-man bobsled to school—a school that Seven informed us was uphill both ways. Seven's grandfather actually invented the four-man bobsled to accommodate his large, growing family. After developing the twelve-man bobsled, his wife instructed him to take up a hobby, for the sole purpose of getting him out of the house more often. We were all quite impressed at his inventiveness and perseverance, to say the least.

The other notable thing about Seven is that, if you were to meet this man on the street (he is a large, beastly man), you would never guess that he is one of the finest yodelers that his country has ever produced. Haunting, mysterious, and always emotional, each yodel tells a story about his far-away homeland. At first, the guys found this very distracting while watching the big game, but we came to accept it as an outlet for Seven to deal with his homesickness.

When we took the time to imagine what hardship and strife he was yodeling about, we were sometimes moved to tears, although none of us knew why. Several of the guys, including my bother-in-law Wally, took yodeling lessons from Seven for a nominal fee. Now we are privileged to have numerous people telling the most tragic stories that you have ever heard during intermissions of the hockey game.

We noticed that Seven never partook in the eating of chicken wings, and after a while, we sensed something was bothering him. He answered our questions with a particularly sensitive and moving yodel that included clucking and quacking noises. When pressed for an explanation, Seven finally told us that back in his native Sweden, there is an outdoor activity where men, carrying high powered rifles, cross-country ski for a long distance. They would then stop, shoulder their firearm, and blast away at chickens and ducks that roamed freely in the woods. While some of his countrymen called it a sport, Seven called it a senseless slaughter. These sportsmen would like to see it gain enough popularity to have it accepted as a Winter Olympic event. Even now, far away from home, his dreams are marked with the soft sounds of skis on the snow, a bang-bang, followed by muffled clucking and quacking, finally fading away to empty nothingness. This seemed to be a truly heavy, emotional burden for any man to bear—even for a large, meaty Swede such as Seven.

This episode affected each and every one of us down at the local sports bar. It touched us deeply. No longer were we sheltered from one of life's deadliest horrors—the callous disregard of any living creature. Although we were not affected enough to give up chicken wings, we were especially attentive whenever Seven did the chicken yodel. While we still couldn't yodel to save our souls, we were waiting for the easy parts that we could partake in. Yes, every once in a while, the bar would reverberate with loud clucking and quacking sounds, and even the flapping of wings could be seen. To witness fully grown men weeping, quacking, and flapping can be a truly touching thing.

The poor waitresses were crying so hard that they could barely stand up; eventually crawling to the back room until the mood lightened. It's not all fun and games down at the local sports bar. We married males have deep emotional roots, and in the proper setting, we are not afraid to show them.

Seven worked tirelessly to translate *The Primer* into Swedish. He was unable to complete this arduous task and commented, "It is much too important a work to be rushed, and our desperate married males back home will be impressed with its perfection."

Seven reported on his progress every week at the local sports bar, and this prince of a man would accept no payment, except for a free beer every twenty minutes or so.

Our Swedish friend has left us now; he has gone back to his homeland. He has left us, taking memories, friendships, and a generous donation from all of us for his newly developed, "Adopt a Duck" program. We wish him well in his quest for righteous justice.

Before he departed, Seven informed me that he had a friend from Finland who would be more than happy to take up the translation where he left off. This does indeed excite me. First, a country near Ethiopia, and now a small island in the South Pacific—there are truly no boundaries for *The Young Male's Marriage Primer* (TYMMP).

When the visitor from Finland showed up at the sports bar, the guys were immediately drawn to him. He turned out to be a fine young man and with a little prodding, he shared some wonderfully touching stories of his homeland. His name was Bjorn, and I had to get my wife, who, as you know, is an accomplished speller, to help me get his name spelt correctly for *The Primer*.

What an amazing coincidence that Bighorn shared his problems with us, as his friend Seven had. He too proved to be a powerful yodeler as well. His concern was for the well being of their national mammal, the elephant walrus seal. He departed for his homeland with a promise to translate *The Primer* when he found the time. Bighorn also collected a generous donation from all the guys to help save this endangered animal. He left with our solemn promise that we would boycott this very same bar if his national mammal, the elephant walrus seal, ever made it to the menu. I firmly believe that we are strong enough morally to make that sacrifice, unless elephant walrus seal meat turns out to be quite tasty.

The success of *The Primer* has humbled me. I have been incredibly fortunate, and I wanted to share my good fortune with others. However, I did not know how to give back to my community and to the rest of the free world. I was watching a golf tournament one day, and it was announced that a golfer named Tiger Woods had set up a foundation to help others less fortunate. This was what I was looking for; I would establish my own charity organization, just like this Tiger fellow.

I called it "The Tiger Woods Foundation," at least I did until Wally pointed out that it would not be fair to this Mr. Woods when my organization took off and surpassed his. This made good sense, and "The Dr. Murray Dick Foundation" was born.

My first triumphant endeavour addressed a problem that I recently researched on a couple of talk shows. Marriages were falling apart not only here in Canada, but globally as well. I felt compelled to do something about this.

"Amateur Marriage Doctors without Borders" is a totally nonprofit organization (it doesn't make any money, just like *The Primer*), spanning the globe to provide quality marriage doctoring at a low, low price. When the lucky applicant pays a small personal fee, plus round-trip airfare, accommodations and beverages, Wally and I will fly in, assess the problems, and guarantee a rock-solid solution to all marriage difficulties before we leave. And make no mistake about it; we will not leave until we have accomplished our goal. We especially want to hear from dying marriages in the southern parts of Florida during our cold Canadian winters. Wally informs me that divorces are rampant down there during this time of year.

The next order of business on the foundation's agenda was the Dr. Murray Dick Book-of-the-Month Club. Again, I had observed this concept on a talk show and I felt our little rural town was ready for such an undertaking.

Because *The Primer* does not have its own talk show as yet, I approached the local library to see if they could host my new endeavour. The librarian, although very surprised to see me, was utterly thrilled with the concept, welcoming any attempt at promoting reading among the married men of our small town. I responded that I was pretty excited myself just being in a library, and I had no idea that there were so many books.

We were firming up the details of our first book-club night when we hit a snag. I asked about the menu, and it was brought to my attention that the library does not, and never has, served chicken wings. They don't even own a deep fryer! On top of that, they do not have satellite-dish TV, and therefore, are not capable of pulling in any sports – if and when the book got dull.

Needless to say, I was disappointed, and I told the librarian that she could draw more people with a better menu and at least some sort of entertainment. Before departing, I asked her if she was aware of my soon-to-be award winning *Primer*, and would she like a copy for the library. She replied that yes, she had heard rumours of this so-called book, and no, she could not accept a copy. She went on to say that if she accepted one from me, she would have to accept a copy from every dunderhead that came around with an amateur marriage manual. I replied that this made good sense to me.

Never one to be discouraged by total failure, and relying on my dogged determination, I pressed on, and eventually the Book-of-the-Month Club found a home at the local sports bar. It seemed like a good fit, the necessary refreshments and entertainment were available for the club patrons when they grew tired of reading, which was quite quickly as it turned out.

The Club started with a splendid literary classic, the fall and winter catalogue from the Tools 'R Us Store. My brother-in-law Wally sponsored this reading. He faithfully went to the store everyday and made off with a new catalogue until he was caught and arrested. Without sufficient copies for everyone, some of us had to double-up to follow along. There was also the problem of chicken wing sauce getting all over the copies, making them tough to read after a while, but the guys were actually reading.

Because the Book Club was my gift to the community, the next selection was my own literary classic, *The Young Male's Marriage Primer*. Although it was hockey season, the bar patrons reluctantly agreed, and the club started with selected readings between periods of the game. I believe that we all grew intellectually from this exercise.

All in all, the club was a huge success, and also a great learning tool for the guys at the bar. For example, it instructed the average married male in the proper usage of a bookmark—something that has never been taught. But as one man pointed out, "I've never needed a bookmark because I know where I left off. It's the part of the magazine that folds out." He has a point.

There is a wise, old saying that I just recently made up, "If your work is being read fifty years from now, you can claim to be a great author." Judging by the reading speed of some of my friends, I believe that I will be able to make this claim.

Take a Kid to Camp was my next charitable undertaking and would have been a worthy endeavour, had not the local health authorities shut down the entire camp until they found the origin of the foul odour. Someone suggested that a few mattresses were the culprits. After I took a quick tour through the facility, I suggested setting fire to the whole bunch.

It was too late to refund the money and the children were all set for some summer fun, so Take a Kid to the Local Sports Bar was set into motion. Please understand that under no circumstances are we condoning underage drinking. These young people are required by sports bar regulations to wear special camp hats that tell the bartenders that they are not to be served. The kids, however, are more than welcome to buy some chicken wings for their sponsor using their tuck-shop dollars, and anyone over sixteen is encouraged to bring a driver's license with him. Without going into detail, let me point out that there is a wealth of vital life experience to be learned here, and forgive me for bragging, but last Super Bowl Sunday I sponsored three young lads of driving-age myself.

My giving nature is never more apparent or meaningful than my latest plan—Power Tools for the Storage-Challenged. It's a sad fact of life that some married males have no place to store their power tools, and my newly designed program addresses this critical need.

First, I allow the fortunate applicants to purchase their own tools, often accompanying them to the store and helping in the selection process.

Then, in an act of unparalleled unselfishness, I offer my workshop as a place to store their new tools due to their lack of workspace. This is not just for the short term; I will provide a home for their brand new power tools forever and ever. Whenever those without tool-sheds feel like doing some woodworking, they can drive over to my shop and proceed to use their very own toys. Although this program is geared mainly for apartment dwellers, those unfortunates, who are not allowed to play with power tools, are more than welcome to apply for membership. To keep their intentions a secret, I will personally pick up the husbands in an old van with, "Strip-Joint Shuttle Bus" painted on the sides. Their wives will never know the true purpose of their absence.

As you can see, I am busier than ever, and my dream is that every single person in our small, rural community is touched by the kindness of my foundation. And you folks, down in southern Florida, don't forget that come next January, I wouldn't mind touching a few of you in person. Wally and I have both purchased matching Bermuda shorts.

And finally, let me say a few words to the Young Male. Let me say thank you for your participation, for following along in the lessons, and for practicing the revolutionary, cutting-edge techniques put forward by *The Primer*. If I have brought a little bit of sense to a confused mind regarding the problems that await a new bridegroom, then my task here is completed. And take heart in the fact that new problems, with new solutions, are an ongoing occurrence in my own marriage and this information will be available in the future.

Yes, Young Males, you did read that right, I mentioned the future. I am already hard at work on *The Primer, Volume Two*. I've known about this for months but until recently, I have been unable to find the strength to tell my dear wife. I was afraid that her pride and joy would betray her, and by now, everyone should know how emotional she can be.

I asked her to join me at the kitchen table, and with both of her hands clasped in mine, I announced that I was writing another amateur marriage manual to further help the less fortunate couples of the world. She looked at me and looked at our hands still wrapped in a precious embrace. My wife slowly raised her eyes until they met mine, and she gave me that look; a special look reserved for only me and only at special times such as this. She tried to speak, but her vocabulary had betrayed her, as has happened so often in the past. She could find no words to express her happiness and joy. The emotion, building deep down within her soul, was already taking control of her lovely, feminine vocal chords. With a pained, bewildered look on her face, she rose to her feet, disentangled her hands from mine, and slowly walked down to the bedroom.

I think she went down there to cry.

Free Bonus Offer

Log on to the amateur marriage doctor's website and get a free lesson pertaining to one of several marital problems that Dr. Murray Dick has encountered and solved. Visit his website on a regular basis to find out how he has messed up lately. Revel in his cutting-edged, revolutionary methods and techniques.

Logon now: www.theyoungmalesmarriageprimer.com

"Is Your Marriage Teetering On the Periphery of Failure?"

Dr. Murray Dick Danby can spot this and point it out to you. He will also explain what a periphery is. His entire married life (35, or 37 years), has been one big "teeter."

Logon now: www.theyoungmalesmarriageprimer.com

"Do You Lack the Minimum Number of Power Tools Needed to Qualify for a Successful Marriage?"

The amateur marriage doctor can show you that a large collection of power tools can actually enhance the love between you and your wife. It is a basic, proven principal; the more tools, the more love. (Quality tools equate to quality love.)

Logon now: www.theyoungmalesmarriageprimer.com

BUY A SHARE OF THE FUTURE IN YOUR COMMUNITY

These certificates make great holiday, graduation and birthday gifts that can be personalized with the recipient's name. The cost of one S.H.A.R.E. or one square foot is $54.17. The personalized certificate is suitable for framing and will state the number of shares purchased and the amount of each share, as well as the recipient's name. The home that you participate in "building" will last for many years and will continue to grow in value.

Here is a sample SHARE certificate:

YES, I WOULD LIKE TO HELP!

I support the work that Habitat for Humanity does and I want to be part of the excitement! As a donor, I will receive periodic updates on your construction activities but, more importantly, I know my gift will help a family in our community realize the dream of homeownership. **I would like to SHARE in your efforts against substandard housing in my community!** *(Please print below)*

PLEASE SEND ME _____ SHARES at $54.17 EACH = $ $_____

In Honor Of: _____

Occasion: (Circle One)   HOLIDAY   BIRTHDAY   ANNIVERSARY

        OTHER: _____

Address of Recipient: _____

Gift From: _____ *Donor Address:* _____

Donor Email: _____

I AM ENCLOSING A CHECK FOR $ $_____ PAYABLE TO HABITAT FOR HUMANITY <u>OR</u> PLEASE CHARGE MY VISA OR MASTERCARD *(CIRCLE ONE)*

Card Number _____ Expiration Date: _____

Name as it appears on Credit Card _____ Charge Amount $ _____

Signature _____

Billing Address _____

Telephone # Day _____ Eve _____

PLEASE NOTE: Your contribution is tax-deductible to the fullest extent allowed by law.
Habitat for Humanity • P.O. Box 1443 • Newport News, VA 23601 • 757-596-5553
www.HelpHabitatforHumanity.org

Printed in the USA
CPSIA information can be obtained
at www.ICGtesting.com
JSHW082207140824
68134JS00014B/479